The Man With
A Time Portal
In His Hat

Kobayaashi

The Man With
A Time Portal
In His Hat

Jai Kobayaashi Gomer

Kobayaashi

First Edition.
First Printing 2022.

Published by Kobayaashi Studios.
www.kobayaashi.co.uk
All enquiries : info@kobayaashi.co.uk

The '*upturned K*' logo is a TradeMark of Kobayaashi Studios.
Cover Design & Artwork by Jai Kobayaashi Gomer.

ISBN : 978-1-914949-07-4

This story is dedicated to love, and to the hope of love, for such is the meaning of life...

'May Time be your friend'
Happy reading,

**

Foreword :

For those purists amongst you who might stand aghast at the seeming inaccuracies of History and known reality contained in these pages, it should be noted that the events taking place here do so in a world much like our own, but not entirely so, much as alluded to by the Atomists of Ancient Greece, among them the philosopher Chrysippus, who theorised that the world itself fragmented, died and was reborn within each moment, offering a vision of a multitude of realities existing either contemporaneously or across the infinite bounds of Time - a notion expanded upon across the ages, most notably by scientists such as Erwin Schrödinger, and many authors of popular Science Fiction...

**

**

When people speak of Percival Ray, it's usually to wonder what drove him to jump from the roof of the Harlequin Hotel on that beautiful summer's day.

His subsequent disappearance is something people tend to *not* talk about...

**

Percival Ray is taking afternoon tea at the Harlequin Hotel. He ponders on the day.

The sky is a most intoxicating shade of deep, cerulean blue. The sun is shining down from a cloudless expanse, the air is clean and sweet, and the calls of summer birds sing out along the town's wide, tree-lined avenues. Citizens young and old are delighting in the miraculous day, the older ones sitting, the lovers promenading and the children racing about with unabashed joy.

It truly is a beautiful day.

Despite that, however, Percival's face is creased with tear-stained sorrow. This is a face which seems to have had its body's heart ripped out through it. It's like somebody had punched Percival in the face *really* hard, and then clawed through the skin and bone to reach down into his body and remove that crushed, devastated organ.

That's how sad he looks.

The light streaming in through the freshly washed and polished windows creates a rainbow on the lace tablecloth, and a smaller bow in the steam slowly rising from the teapot. The well-presented display of bite-sized cakes and temptingly-delicious sandwiches do nothing to raise his spirits. Even the Battenberg leaves him cold. Even the Battenberg.

That's how sad he is.

He is sad because he has lost the love of his life. He has lost all hope in love, and he almost wishes that he'd never encountered it in the first place.

Except, he would never wish to have never met *her*. She was the only sweetness in his life, and if the price of having known her is the pain of losing her, then so be it. He is ready to pay that price, albeit for a brief moment.

Brief only, because Percival has decided to end his life.

**

The Harlequin Hotel is an architectural marvel. It was designed in 1829 by the renowned artist Ernest Underbotham, famous mostly for the 'walking' buildings of Calella, North of Barcelona, which were built for The Great Exhibition of London in 1851, and are still walking today. Ernest had a fascination for the unusual and the unexpected, and so it was that he designed the Harlequin Hotel to feature an intricate network of finely-sculpted spiral metal staircases, both within and around the structure. Many led nowhere. Several led to the roof, which offered a view over the avenued centre of this delightful town.

And it is upwards and along one of these delightful staircases that Percival now finds himself spiralling, with each slow, deliberate footstep taking him that much closer to his seemingly-inevitable end.

Every tap of leather sole on painted metal, as each shoe in turn hits a step to propel him roofward, seems to Percival to strike the air much like the ticking of a giant clock. Every tick another second closer to his demise, and the ending of the pain which tortures his every waking moment, and has done since he realised that he had lost her for good, and that nothing he could do could ever bring her back to him.

Tick.

Round and round the spiral winds. Onwards and upwards Percival steps.

Tick.

Until the bright cacophony of voices from the street is softened by the summer breeze and the chatter of rooftop birds.

Tick.

And Percival steps out onto the roof, and calmly heads to the low stone wall at its edge.

No ordinary stone wall, of course. Ernest Underbotham's creation is capped by a sculpture of the town's skyline as could be seen beyond it at the time the Hotel was built. On every side, the wall is a lasting image of the town as it stood over a hundred years ago. It presents to the viewer a physical history of buildings which no longer exist, and is contrasted by sections of altered skyline beyond the roof, where progress has changed the town. It is a remarkable crown befitting this unique structure.

And here, at the edge of the roof, stands Percival, staring out at the town.

At first, none of the figures passing by along the streets five floors below see the young man, as he calmly steps onto the low, sculpted wall which serves as a border between the roof and the not-roof. It takes a few seconds for him to be noticed - those few seconds in which Percival steels himself to make his final step from life to death.

Suddenly, a shout rises from the street, and people look up from their lives just in time to see Percival step out...

**

**

Percival's journey to the air beyond the rooftop of the Harlequin Hotel began three months prior to that fateful day.

He was twenty one years and three months of age at that time. He was an earnest worker, always correct - polite, well-dressed, not quite charming, but always ready to help or compliment others. Percival was pleasant. He was not a riot. He was not passionately loved, but neither was he disliked by anybody. He was merely a very nice young man.

He had spent three years working at the accounting firm of Battersey, Battersey & Kendrick in Cornbury, Cambridgeshire, located in what used to be the town's jewellery district - though that industry had fallen into decline some decades prior, and it was the accountancy industry which had revitalised the area, bringing in a new, younger population and the latest fashions from across the Empire.

Percival was proud to be an accountant, albeit only a Grade 3 Under-Novice. He was still a part of the world's greatest industry, one on which the business community from London to Calcutta to Darwin in the Antipodes relied to keep their wheels turning. How else would commerce thrive, and merchants earn, if there were not accountants on hand to record and analyse transactions, to work out monies owed, fees payable or taxes required from the untold millions of sales and financial investments made every day? Finance was like a whirlwind, and accountants were the brave warriors who challenged that deadly vortex, standing tall in the face of overwhelming chaos, ready with quill and abacus to draw its power down into precise columns of pounds, shillings and pence, where it would lie in perpetuity, tamed into stillness by the hands of Man.

Mondays to Saturdays were workdays - accountants were known for their all-in, gung-ho work ethic, but even *they* took Sundays off. Sundays were for savouring life, for relaxing, promenading, engaging in conversation or the ever-so subtle art of courting.

Sundays were also the days when Percival was confronted with the notion that what he lacked in life, was love. How he envied those about him who spent their Sundays parading, cavorting, or sitting in the screen-lit shadows of the cinema, stealing kisses and bringing romance to life. How he longed to find that right woman, the one who would eagerly love him, and be loved by him in return.

In the meantime, Percival hunted for treasure - or, more accurately, treasures. On his Sundays he would scour the curiosity shops and flea markets of the old town, exploring the meandering medieval alleyways, hoping to find something beautiful, something delicious, or something which carried with it a tale which reeked of adventure and life.

Often, he returned empty-handed, or with some knick-knack which would take pride of place on one of the shelves in the living room of his suitably-sufficient rented accommodation for a brief moment, before being swiftly hidden by time and a lack of attention. Occasionally, however, he would come across some great discovery which would delight him for days.

One time, he spotted the most exquisite artwork in the shadows of a rambling shop which was filled to its twisted wooden rafters with the old and the forgotten. It was a portrait in oils of a young man, much the same in appearance as Percival - the same chin, even the same faraway look in his eyes, as though searching for some adventure which lay just out of reach. It was only later, when researching the artist, that Percival discovered that the young man in the painting was in fact his great-grandfather, Elias Percival Ray. That painting - small, and worn with time as it was - still held pride of place on his living room wall, just above the fire, gazing out across the room to the world beyond.

It was on a Sunday, at the beginning of summer, that Percival's life was to be changed forever.

It was a crisp, bright morning, carrying with it a memory of the cold spring which had just passed, and also a promise of the warmer days to come. It was a day of possibilities.

Percival had been paid the week previous, and his bank account was fat with credit, to the tune of over two hundred pounds. This was to last him the Quarter, of course, but nevertheless, he was free to shop for treasures that Sunday without a care.

And so he did.

He began his morning, as was often the case, with a Turkish coffee served at a table on the cobble-stoned pavement outside The Gibbet Coffee House. There he sat, savouring the drink's aroma and thick, bitter taste, while watching the world and his lover amble past.

After that, he took a walk through what are charmingly known by the locals as "The Souks". True, they have the feel of some of the old-town markets of places such as Marrakech or Damascus - though few of the residents of Cornbury had ever travelled to such places, instead encountering their like only in books, or at the cinema. It's said that these time-worn markets were given the moniker by an old sailor who had travelled widely, and who had visited the town on a whim, and that the name just stuck.

It is also said that one can find anything in The Souks, if one just happens to look in the right shop window at the right time, and so it was that Sunday morning as Percival scoured for delights through every twist and turn of the ancient alleyways.

He pondered as he walked, that the labyrinthine pathways of the Souks were much the same as the routes a man takes through his life, whereby the decisions made at any particular point had the possibility to open up a world of exciting treasures, or hide them from view, never to be encountered. There are places within them where one might be forced to choose from three, four or even more pathways to depart from a particular location. So many decisions, and no way of knowing where any particular road might lead.

On that day, they led to the Curios Quarter, a place teeming with shops and stalls containing almost every thing imaginable. Here one might find an ancient Egyptian scarab beetle, preserved for all time in a small jar, or a dozen left boots tied together with an old piece of string for luck. Or some handcrafted candleholders. Or a box filled with old, abandoned toys. Or the keys to a dead man's house.

Once there, Percival wandered into a shop which he'd never visited before. It wasn't new, it was just unvisited by him. It seemed to be a place which had always been there, waiting.

Percival wandered through the cramped aisles, overflowing with the strange, the bizarre and the history-laden mundane. He casually stroked some of the shelves as he passed along them, touching one thing, then another. Occasionally he stopped to pick up an item, before carefully replacing it in the same spot, taking pains to position it entirely within the footprint it had left in the dust.

While reaching for one shiny little trinket at the back of a shelf, Percival's hand brushed past the stiff fur felt of an old hat. He reached for the hat, in order to move it out of his way, and was struck immediately by how familiar the sensation seemed to be of holding it. He turned it over in his hands, unsure as to why he would be drawn to something so unspectacular, yet the attraction itself was undeniable.

He did not care for hats, usually. This was one thing which set him apart from many of his contemporaries. The wearing of hats was rather in vogue then - and not much has changed in the three months since - yet Percival did not consider himself the hat type.

And yet, there was something about this piece of rough felt, which was in dire need of some care and seemed to have suffered a little from having been stuck on a long-forgotten shelf for rather too much time. The grosgrain ribbon was a little tatty, as was the trim around the brim, but it possessed a certain elegance despite these imperfections.

Percival decided to buy the hat. He spent some time locating the shopkeeper, before requesting a price for it.

"Oh my," said the shopkeeper, delighted to see the hat, it seemed. "The old Homburg! I'd quite forgotten that. An exquisite piece of millinery, I must say." The shopkeeper then reached out with one hand, and stroked the old felt. "Quite exquisite."

"Indeed," said Percival. "And I'm sure you could tell me all about how much this hat means to you, or how perhaps it was worn by some great personage or other, and you couldn't possibly sell it for a measly amount, but I should tell you that I'm no easy mark. It is, after all, just a hat."

"On the contrary, sir. This is not just a hat. Far from it, indeed."

"Then I'm sure you would have me believe that this hat was once possessed by one of the great heroes of past times? Perhaps the Duke of some such, or the Lord of another?"

"Hardly. This hat has been worn by one gentleman only, and has spent much of its existence gathering dust on the shelf where you found it."

"Then what, I'd like to know, makes this hat worthy of such effusive praise?"

"It is not the hat itself sir, but what it contains," said the shopkeeper.

Percival turned the hat over again in his hands. It still felt like a delight to hold, but he could see that it contained nothing. "This hat is empty," he said.

"Right now, that does seem to be the case," replied the shopkeeper, "but when you least expect it, it will show you something remarkable." He leaned closer to Percival, and whispered in a conspiratorial, hushed tone, "This hat, when it chooses, opens up a portal to other hats in other times."

"What on Earth do you mean, 'in other times'?"

"I mean, sir, that this hat occasionally becomes a portal to the past, which opens itself into hats across the ages."

"Are you mad, man? That you'd believe I'd consider such poppycock!" Percival was rather offended.

"Not at all, sir. In fact, I shall offer you the hat on a trial basis. If by the month's end you find you are merely in possession of an old, worn hat with no redeeming features, you may keep or discard it as you wish, with no charge employed. If, however, you discover this to be all that I say, you will return here and pay me... ten pounds for the hat."

"Ten pounds? For a hat?"

"No, sir. Ten pounds for a hat containing a gateway to Time itself."

Percival considered the offer. It was rather ludicrous, but he had nothing to lose from the transaction, and so he agreed to the terms, shaking hands with the shopkeeper and promising to return at the end of the month with ten pounds if, indeed, the hat showed the inclination to open a portal to the past.

If it did not, he would have a free hat. Percival was rather pleased with himself, and so headed back through the Souks to the Gibbet, and treated himself to another cup of deliciously-thick Turkish coffee.

The rest of that Sunday passed without incident. Percival enjoyed a stroll around the town - for once, fully-behatted - then in the evening he bought a ticket to watch "Cities on the Moon", a classic science fiction film at the cinema. It was one of the early films, made in black and white, and coloured by hand. Percival so admired the artistry of those who created such things. For an hour, it seemed as though he was actually transported to the surface of the Moon, and the fabulous cities built there.

Of course, he knew that no cities had yet been built on the Moon's surface - in fact, the settlements which had in actuality been built there could scarcely be called villages - but it *was* a fascinating and immersive escape into the fantasy of the film's makers, and Percival thoroughly enjoyed himself.

He returned home happy with his day, and put the hat aside.

**

It was not until several days later that Percival remembered the hat he had bought. He was about to leave home for work on the Wednesday morning when he spotted it, lounging on a bookshelf as though making itself at home. He tried it on, and thought that, despite its tattiness, he would wear it to work that day as an amusement.

His fellow-workers at Battersey, Battersey & Kendrick were indeed most amused. They were not used to seeing Percival in a hat, and for a short while it was the subject of animated discussion. But then the bell rang, and each worker headed to their desk to begin the day's work. Percival put the hat in a drawer in his desk, and turned his attention to the files filled with numbers, which were arranged before him.

At lunchtime, when the bell rang once more, most of the workers headed for the cafeteria on the ground floor of the company building. There, they enjoyed subsidised meals which were more than adequate, and loud interdepartmental socialising. Percival, however, preferred to eat by himself at his desk, and would bring in his own food. He was not anti-social, he merely preferred to eat alone, and in silence.

That day he had brought a salad sandwich, and two thick

slices of Battenberg cake. He had also brought a flask filled with tea. White. No sugar. He sat in silence, and enjoyed his lunch.

It was while he was enjoying the second slice of cake that Percival heard strange sounds coming from within his desk drawer. Sure that he was imagining this, he opened the drawer. There was little in there but for the hat, but it did seem that the sounds - of traffic, of crowds in a city - had become louder and more clear once he'd opened the drawer.

Percival picked up the hat, and turned it over in his hands, as he'd done a number of times before.

Only this time, the hat was not empty.

Rather, inside the bowl of the hat was the top of a person's head, as though Percival was looking down at what would be the inside of another hat, with the owner's head still firmly ensconced within its bounds.

Shocked, Percival let out a cry, and flung the hat aside. Surely, he thought, this was a hallucination - perhaps brought on by stress, or overwork? But he suffered from neither, so that could not be the case. Perhaps he had come down with a fever, with no signs or warning? But he did not seem to be sick, and could think of no other reason why he would see another person's head inside his hat that made any kind of sense.

But then there was a voice, emanating from the hat. Calling out from within.

Carefully, and with trepidation, Percival reached out, and picked up the hat.

Where should have been the inside of the crown of the hat there was instead the face of a young man, he holding his own hat in turn, and looking through at Percival.

On seeing Percival's face peering back at him, the man uttered a shriek, and made a move as if he were to throw down the hat.

"No, please," Percival called out, in earnest. "Please don't go."

"Qui êtes vous?" asked the man in the hat. "Comment est-ce que vous êtes dans mon chapeau?"

Though the man spoke quickly, and with a rough tone, Percival knew enough French to understand that this new visitor, visible only within the bounds of the rim of the Homburg, was as confused about this millinery upset as Percival himself.

"I'm sorry, je ne sais pas, my friend," answered Percival.

The man proceeded to rattle off French in a fast-flowing, guttural manner, leaving Percival flummoxed.

"Please! S'il vous plaît! Sir, you need to slow down. I'm afraid I'm unable to understand you, and if you don't mind me saying so, your tone is becoming rather aggressive."

"Agressif?" The man exploded, his face distorted with incandescent rage. He began to spit indecipherable words and phrases at a rapid-fire pace at a discombobulated Percival, the volume of his voice rising with his temper until he furiously thrust an arm through the hat, grabbed Percival's shirt collar, and began to shake him vigorously.

Percival was shocked. He shrieked, grabbing at this alien hand - this unwarranted and unrequested invasion into his reality and his personal space.

"Unhand me, you bloody brute!" he cried, as he attempted to prise the coarse fingers from his collar.

At that moment, Percival heard raised voices, and realised that the crowds were heading back from lunch at the cafeteria, and would soon reach the office. He was under no illusions that they would find his current situation anything other than terrifyingly unprofessional. Some deep, primal part of his brain made the decision to grab the hand, and bite it. Hard.

With an enraged cry, the Frenchman released his grip, pulling his hand back into the world to which it belonged. As he did so, Percival pulled open his desk drawer and shoved the hat inside, before slamming the drawer shut just as the first workers arrived in the office.

Though he was shaking inside with shock and bemusement, Percival nonetheless attempted to radiate a sense of calmness as he assembled the remnants of his lunch, and set them neatly aside, so that he could begin the afternoon's work.

In truth, because he was not a riot, nor passionately loved, nor disliked by anybody - because he was merely *a very nice young man*, nobody paid him any mind. Nobody noticed the flush in his face, or the trembling which had overtaken his fingers. It was without shock or fanfare that the bell rang, and the workforce entered once more into the tasks for which they were employed.

The afternoon passed in a blur, and Percival was sure that he had made countless errors in the mathematical operations he carried out, but it was all he could do not to cry out loud, to wail and shake. Instead, he waited until the final bell rang, and remained at his desk, busying himself with nothingness until the last stragglers had left the office, before taking a deep breath and reaching out a trembling hand to grasp the handle of the desk's drawer.

But, for the longest time, his shaking fingers would not pull on the handle, and the drawer remained closed. Percival squeezed his eyes shut, and groaned aloud, the sound echoing loudly in the empty office. Then, in one swift movement, he yanked open the drawer and pulled out the hat, slamming it down on the desk.

Once again, he took a deep breath, steeling himself to open his eyes and look at the crumpled Homburg held tightly in his fist. He couldn't hear any sound coming from it, so that eased his mind somewhat, but it still took several more seconds for him to open his eyes, and look down.

And there, on the desk, was the hat.

No irate Frenchman, no other worlds - and no angry, grasping hands reaching through to try to throttle him.

Just a hat.

Delicately, Percival reached inside and pressed at the fabric, seeking to convince himself that the danger had passed and that he need not be afraid.

It was just a hat.

With apparent calmness, Percival collected his belongings - the leftover wrapping of his lunch, his half-empty flask and one dishevelled hat - and left the office, his footsteps loud in the silence of the empty room.

Down the stairs, and out into the evening streets. Through the thinning crowds of workers making their way home, until he reached his own door.

Only once he'd entered his home and locked the door behind him did he collapse, and finally allow himself to give in to the pent-up trauma caused by the day's events, and quietly sob.

**

The next day, Thursday, Percival did not go to work. Instead, he telephoned his office manager and reported that he was suffering from a slight fever. The manager was concerned more with finding someone to cover the vacant desk for the day than with the state of Percival's health, and thus the conversation was a short one.

And so, while the office was filling up with Accountants of various grades, all eager to tame the numbers of the world, Percival sat at his dining table, staring at the hat.

It had not shown signs of life since the previous day's uncomfortable encounter, but he was still wary of it, nervous that it might re-open a dastardly portal to some deranged French maniac - or something manifestly worse.

Instead, the hat sat silent and still on the table, and the room was quiet but for the muted sounds of outside life as others went about their days, oblivious to Percival's unusual situation.

After much contemplation, Percival reached out and picked up the quietly menacing headpiece. He turned it over in his hands, as he'd done before without consequence, and to his relief, it remained just a hat.

As he sat and pondered, fingers grazing the rough felt, Percival began to relax, and found himself able at last to view his experience without the bias of fear or upset.

He recollected the unsettling sensation of finding another person within the bounds of the Homburg, but this time with a sense of wonder which had been overwhelmed at the time.

Another person. Possibly another country. Perhaps even another time. This really had been quite magical, quite remarkable. Percival was certain that few people had experienced something quite so bizarre as having a man reach through a hat, across bounds of Time and Space, with the furious intention of strangling them.

Just the thought of it made Percival chuckle lightly to himself. It really was quite absurd.

That afternoon, Percival went for a walk. It was rather invigorating, walking through the daytime streets on a day other than Sunday. There were far fewer people out and about, as most were at work, whether in offices or shops or factories. The few left to wander through the wide, crowd-free avenues were pre-school children and those accompanying them, food vendors re-positioning their carts in plenty of time for the post-work rush, and street cleaners, brushes purposefully in hand, working with the proud diligence warranted by their historical profession.

Somehow, the air seemed cleaner, the sounds of birdsong more crisp. There was a hint of a skip in the step of young Percival Ray.

Soon, he was seated at a table on the cobblestones outside the Gibbet Coffee House, enjoying the delicious aroma of a hitherto-unexplored blend of freshly-ground coffee beans, while watching the occasional passers-by pass by.

It had become a most delightful day.

At that moment, Percival decided that it was only right and correct to pay the shopkeeper for the hat. After all, he had been truthful in his assertion - the Homburg did indeed contain a portal through Time, albeit a somewhat unnerving one.

He checked his wallet, and counted out only a few coins, barely six shillings and change. He owed the shopkeeper ten pounds. The bank was nearby, and so Percival decided he would withdraw the entire ten pounds and head into the Curios Quarter, which he did.

Despite the brightness of the day, the streets of the Souks were in perpetual shade. The narrow, winding alleyways permitted little light to reach down to the level of the old, cobbled streets, worn smooth over time and by the traversing footsteps of so many lives.

His feet drew him on, knowing the way better than he, and soon Percival reached the entrance to the curious curio store, and entered. The doorbell rang with a delicate tone to announce his arrival.

From across the crowded, shelf-lined floor, Percival could see that the shopkeeper was busy with a customer, and so he held back, absently investigating the tiers of random, possibly-magical trinkets and gewgaws.

After some minutes had passed, however, Percival grew impatient. He pulled the crisp ten pound note from his wallet, and prepared to approach the shopkeeper, still mid-discussion with the customer.

Percival cleared his throat softly, wishing to be noticed, but determined also to remain polite. The shopkeeper looked over at him with a smile of recognition, and Percival smiled back.

The customer also looked, and recognised Percival immediately.

The customer was Avarice Davies, a fellow-worker from the office at Battersey, Battersey & Kendrick, who also smiled when he saw Percival. "Percival! What a delightful surprise!" he called across the floor.

Percival was horrified. He could not possibly bring up

the matter of the time-bending hat in front of his co-worker, let alone recount the story of the enraged Frenchman, or hand over ten pounds for the privilege of having been assaulted in a most unbelievable way. He had no doubt that Davies would enjoy telling this tale upon his return to work, and that he, Percival, would become a laughing stock, and a figure of unwarranted ridicule.

And so, instead, when beckoned over by the shopkeeper, Percival merely asked, quietly and politely, whether the shopkeeper sold snuff. The shopkeeper looked Percival eye-to-eye, and told him that he would check his stock room for any remaining supplies.

Percival then turned to Avarice Davies and acknowledged him. "Davies. So pleased to see you. Will you be returning to the office soon?"

"Soon enough, old man," Davies replied, heartily. "My wrist is almost healed, and so I shall soon be well-equipped to hoist the quill once more. I should no doubt take more care when descending the steps in future, and not hurry to lunch, right?"

"Of course." Percival was not really a man who enjoyed small talk.

"So, what brings you here? I venture it isn't just snuff? Surely you could pick that up from the Gibbet?"

Percival ventured that he wanted to try something a little different from his usual taste, and the idea that this straight-laced young man was seeking to explore the unusual in the minutiae of his life tickled Davies somewhat, and he laughed, delighted.

At that moment, the shopkeeper returned. He looked at Percival pointedly.

"I'm afraid we have no snuff remaining, sir," he said. "Perhaps there is another matter with which I could assist you?"

Their gazes locked for much longer than was called for in a casual conversation, as Percival found himself torn between honesty and the fear of ridicule. Fear won the battle, and Percival was dismayed at the look of disappointment and betrayal in the eyes of the shopkeeper as he mumbled that there was nothing else, and hurried from the shop, eyes cast down in shame.

Davies called out after him, but Percival barely registered the somewhat informal farewell, and instead rushed blindly into the twisting, turning ginnels of the Souks.

As he hurried through the narrow alleys, the facades on each side seemed to throw back at him the memories of moments before - of his betrayal of the shopkeeper, and the dastardly humiliation of himself. Percival's eyes streamed with angry tears as he strode without care or attention through the blind streets of the Souks, caring neither for a destination nor for the growing pain on the sole of his left foot, which blistered with every regret-laden step.

By the time his tears had dried, and he had been forced to stop marching on account of the pain from the blister, evening had fallen, and the shadows grew thicker in this suddenly-menacing maze.

Percival stopped at a low stone wall around an old well, and sat while he removed his sock and shoe to inspect his foot. With every action, he could feel new eyes upon him, staring out from the darkness.

The keepers of a thousand shops and stalls were locking away their wares for the night, and the gentle murmuration of idly shopping crowds had dissipated. The quaint novelty of the Souks' antiquity suddenly became rather threatening. Percival replaced his sock and shoe, and faced the urge to flee.

Unfortunately, he had no idea where he was. He'd raced through unknown streets in a bid to lose himself and hide from his guilt, and he had succeeded in one of his endeavours - he had let himself get well and truly lost.

He looked around, and saw that there were four exits from the tiny plaza in which he found himself. Four darkening alleyways. At the corners of two of those, young men gathered, speaking softly among themselves and glancing occasionally in his direction. At another, a young woman leaned seductively against the cool stone wall, gazing directly at Percival, her tongue slowly moistening her lips.

The fourth exit was empty of people. There was nothing there but cold, dark shadow.

Percival knew that he had to make a choice, and quickly, for late evening was swiftly becoming night.

He took a breath, and began to walk calmly, but with determination, to the fourth exit. As he did so, one of the men at one of the other entrances stepped forward.

"My friend," he called out, with just a hint of an accent.

Percival froze, mid-step.

"You don't want to go that way," the young man continued.

"And why not, may I ask?" Percival responded, rather too roughly.

"Because that path leads only to the Tannery Quarter, and there is nothing there at this time of night except for the foul stench of tanners at work." When Percival remained still, the young man said "If you're looking for the nearest exit, head through Heroes Passage, to your left. It's only a minute's walk from here."

The man was pointing to the street where the young woman stood relaxing against the wall, now seeming more bored than dangerously seductive. Percival muttered mumbled, guilty thanks and set off through the Passage, vaguely acknowledging the woman as he passed her. "Excuse me, miss," was all he said as he rushed past her to safety.

Less than thirty achingly-long seconds later, Percival reached the world of street lights and smiling faces, and the most welcome aroma of freshly-ground coffee which poured from the Gibbet.

It was there, on the cobble-stoned streets below the glow of sodium lamps, that his knees gave way, and Percival fell to the floor, his very breath trembling. A few fellow pedestrians helped him to his feet, and seated him at a table outside the Gibbet, and soon a grateful Percival was embracing a hot cup of coffee, assuring his saviours that he was in fact well, and that he had merely suffered an unusual spell of exhaustion, and then this became just another night, and there was no danger, and there were no shadows, and the air was scented with exquisite, night-blooming flowers.

**

**

The next morning, Percival woke earlier than usual. He lay there, wrapped in sheets crumpled by a night of restless tossing and turning, and pondered all that had happened to him since the moment he first grazed his hand along the stiff fur felt of the Homburg, from his initial carefree humouring of the shopkeeper to the angry ranting of the Frenchman to the look of disappointment in the eyes of the shopkeeper as Percival lied to his face.

Where only days previously, Percival would have considered himself a happy, lighthearted fellow, now he felt himself heavily-laden with sorrow and troubles. Not least of these was his own self-loathing, now that he had become something so awful and cowardly as a liar.

As he walked to work that Friday morning, he took no joy in the freshness of the air, the chirpiness in the chitter-chatter of birdlife, or the vibrant hum of summer which infused the crowds of workers surging along the pavements with not a care in their workaday worlds.

As he seated himself at his desk, readying himself for the bell, he felt no excitement at the thought of the reams of papers piled high upon his desk, each sheet filled with numbers waiting just for him, so that he might lead them into their appropriate columns, and guide them to where they belonged.

Instead he sat without humour, unsure of himself and his place in the world.

His melancholic reverie was broken by a shout from across the office.

"Percival! My good man, how the Devil are you?"

Percival looked up to see Avarice Davies striding towards him, along with a couple of other fellows Percival knew by face, but could not put a name to.

"As you can see, I'm back," Davies continued, flexing the wrist of one hand. "All healed and ready to take on the world, right?" The man's positivity and zeal were palpable. "So what happened to you yesterday? You left so quickly I thought you'd been bitten by a damned flea!"

The others around Davies laughed at this, and the three of them crowded about Percival's desk, in a conversational huddle such as friends do. "So, out with it, man. Why were you really there? It was not for snuff, to be sure, right?"

Percival sat silently on his chair as the others formed a wall around him. Though he knew he had no reason to do so, he felt uncomfortable - more so as he had no idea how to answer Davies' query. He could hardly blurt out the truth of the time-bending Homburg, or make light of his encounter with the Frenchman. There was nothing to be gained by telling the truth, but to tell a lie would only darken his mood and his soul further. Therefore, Percival remained silent.

"Of course, there was no way you ventured so deeply into the Souks for snuff. Come, you can tell us. We're friends, right?" asked Davies, eyeing Percival intently, though without malice.

"I'll bet he was buying something for a young chickadee," said one of Davies' entourage.

"That sounds about right," added the other.

"Is that true, Percival?" asked Davies with keen interest. "Were you shopping for a sweetheart? Who is she? Tell us her name. Does she work here? Tell us, man. Don't keep us in suspense!"

Percival needed to stop the conversation, but he could find no way of doing so without being impolite, and the good humoured insistence of his new co-conversationalists did not deserve such rudeness. In trying to balance his wants and theirs, he found himself stammering.

"By God, it's true!" exclaimed Davies. "Our man Percival Ray has snagged himself a filly!" This last exclamation was spoken loudly enough to garner attention from desks further afield, and Percival began to worry that the whole office might somehow be dragged into this fiasco, and so in order to end this as quickly and as quietly as possible, Percival declared "Yes. Yes, I am enjoying the company of a young lady. No, she doesn't work here. She - she works at a milliners in... Hempton Lowers, and lives there also. We don't get to meet as often as we'd like, and so I thought I'd surprise her with a trinket."

"My, you're a dark horse aren't you?" asked Davies, and the others chorused a cheerful agreement. "So tell us," Davies continued, "where did you two lovebirds meet?"

Just then, the bell rang, offering Percival some small relief as his new-found friends departed for their own desks, with Davies calling out a final "We'll speak soon, dark horse!" as he retreated. Percival thought his rapidly-beating heart might explode, but it didn't, and he purposely slowed his breathing, calming himself, as he reached for the sheet of paper on the top of the pile closest to him, drowning the images of good-natured terror in pure, emotionless numbers.

The minutes of the morning dragged on into the hours, and the hours passed in a blur until the bell rang for lunch. Percival kept his eyes down as the throng massed, heading past him in a cloud of people-noise on its way to the ground floor cafeteria. For a moment it seemed as though Davies and friends would stop to invite Percival to join them, but they were too engrossed in what appeared to be an amusing conversation, and passed on by without bothering him.

His sandwiches that day were of the cheese and pickle variety. Hearty chunks of cheese, topped with a dollop of delightfully tangy pickle, between two thick slabs of white crusty bread. For dessert, of course, a couple of slices of Battenberg. Percival laid his lunch out neatly on the desk, as always, and poured a cup of tea from his flask.

As he ate his lunch, taking large bites of his thick sandwich, he began to think on how he was perceived by those with whom he spent his working days. The earlier conversation, as disturbing as it was because of his unique situation and the lies he was forced to tell in order to cover up the bizarre truth, had set him as the centre of the attention, and Percival realised that this didn't feel as atrociously bad as he'd assumed it would be. In fact, a small part of him was feeling a spark of delight at being noticed; being heard; being a thing of interest.

He'd never really been one for attention. Even as a child he'd shunned the spotlight, preferring the gentle, quiet neighbourhood of the background, with its lack of drama and noise. But for some reason, he was feeling drawn to... to something. Perhaps he had focused too much recently on being without love in his life that he had not considered his obvious lack of friends.

For a moment he considered the idea of a friendship with Davies and the others, but he quickly remembered that what had drawn them to him was a lie. Not only that, but what had retained their attention was an addition to that lie. Percival knew that to lie was to invite discovery and scorn, therefore so much more so to lie and then compound that lie by wrapping it in another - for, he told himself, lies only remain hidden by being wrapped in the stained, ugly paper of other lies.

Suddenly, his appetite left him.

That afternoon, while the sun shone brightly through the high, arched windows of the office, Percival sat in a shade of his own making. When the final bell rang, he hurried to leave before he could be spoken to by Davies. He rushed through the streets, to his door, and threw himself through it, shutting it firmly behind him and locking the world outside.

**

That night, as the town clock struck eight and the sun edged ever-closer to the horizon, Percival sat at his dining table, empty plate cast aside, watching the colours of the sky melt through blue to red to gold.

Sounds of summer life filled the warm evening air, but all of it came from outside Percival's window. Inside, in the small but well-kept living room, there was only silence, and within that silence was only sadness.

And it was all because of that cursed, troublemaking hat. Percival had a good mind to toss it through the open window, out into the street. In fact, he dashed over to the shelf on which the Homburg lay, grabbed it and rushed to the window, arm raised.

But, for some reason, he could not let it go.

He sat down once again at the table, smoothing out the creases he had made in the fabric by gripping it so tightly. He stroked the fabric softly, as though it were a kitten, and wondered why he could not let this thing go from his life.

"What are you?" he asked the shaped, crafted felt fur headpiece.

"Excuse me?" came the response.

Caught unawares, Percival dropped the hat on the table, before picking it up quickly and turning it over - terrified at what he might see, but unable to stop himself finding out.

Once again, within the bounds of the brim of the hat, this time framed by the finest wisp of lace at a bonnet's edge, there was a face, staring back at him with the same look of stunned incredulity which he wore on his own. Only, this time there was no indignant Frenchman with a penchant for violent fisticuffs, but...

...an angel.

Percival could not speak, only look in awe, as a vision of radiant heavenly beauty stared back at him with the widest of blue eyes, her features so exquisitely delicately drawn so as to catch his very breath and she, gazing back at him as though she felt the same powerful and infinite bond between them, and the two of them held their poses for so long they'd almost forgotten that each was inside the other's headwear, and they both, he and she together, fell immediately, completely and unstoppably in love.

Eventually, he drew enough breath to whisper "Percival," to which she responded softly, "Isabelle." And once more the two of them allowed themselves to be wrapped in the wondrous silence of the moment.

After some long, ecstatic seconds of gazing and being gazed at, each tried to speak, and was caught in the words of the other, their shy interruptedness falling over itself with gay abandon, and they laughed as though they had never laughed before, as though the world was young and they with it, and summer was forever.

Isabelle spoke first.

"Sir," she asked, bringing her face, her most beautiful face, closer to the lace-bordered opening of her bonnet, "may I enquire, how is it that you are in my bonnet? Is this witchery of some sort?"

"No," Percival replied, his eyes never once leaving hers, "at least I don't think so. I'll admit, it is somewhat unusual, to say the least. I mean, it's not every day that one finds another person inside one's hat!"

"Indeed," said Isabelle. "It is the strangest of things. To be honest, such a thing should really terrify a person - to be speaking to another through the medium of their apparel, and yet... I find the sight of you somehow comforting." Isabelle quickly followed this by blurting out "I hope you don't find that too forward! It's just that-"

"I know exactly what you mean," agreed Percival, with urgency. "I feel completely and utterly the same. I feel as though I have been waiting for you for forever, and that this moment was always here, waiting for us."

"You have the heart of a poet... Percival."

"And you make that heart beat faster, Isabelle."

"Tell me," Isabelle asked the love-struck Percival, "has this ever happened to you before?"

And so it was that Percival recounted the tale of the hat, from his discovery of it on a dusty shelf hidden away from the world, to the rather disturbing encounter with the angry Frenchman. He omitted certain details - he did not, for example, tell her of his lie to the shopkeeper, and his ensuing parade of lies told so that the first might not be uncovered.

"And then I turned over the hat, and there you were, and it feels as though every moment of my life was crafted so as to bring me here, now, to be speaking with you from..." Percival trailed off, realising that as strange as this encounter might be, neither had raised the notion that they may inhabit not only different spaces, but different times.

"Isabelle, might I ask - and I know it may sound strange, but we both realise that this encounter is far from ordinary, and- where are you?"

"I am picnicking with my family in the dunes at Holywell Ramparts, but my home is in St Ives. And you?"

"I am quite a distance from you, in Cambridgeshire to be exact."

"My, that is... you seem so clear, I would have imagined you to be closer."

"Indeed. Now, please don't think me a fool, but... might I ask what year it is in St Ives?"

"What year? Well, Percival, we may be half a country away, but we do have the year in common, do we not?"

"I'm not totally certain that we do," replied Percival, and he reminded her of the shopkeeper's assertion that the Homburg contained a portal which traversed Time. "So, tell me. What is the year in which you live?"

"It is seventeen hundred and ninety-four here. When is it with you, sweet Percival?"

Percival's heart sank, and Isabelle saw the emotion wash across his face.

"Oh no, my dear Percival. Is it such a terrible thing? Are we separated by the years? Are they too many? Please tell me the divide is not too great."

Percival sighed, and tears pooled in his eyes. "My dear Isabelle, it is too great indeed. What an utter fool Fate has made of me, of us, to have us meet and... and..."

"...and to fall in love?"

"Yes! And to fall in love, yes, yes, yes my sweet, sweet Isabelle. And to fall in love, while conspiring to separate us by such an ocean of Time."

"How much time, Percival?" asked the most beautiful woman the world had ever seen.

"In my world, the year is nineteen thirty nine. We are... one hundred and forty-five years apart," Percival told her through his tears. "One hundred and forty-five years!"

And Percival and Isabelle gazed into one another's eyes as they shared a moment of deepest sadness and loss.

Though they had known one another only through a tiny portal, and then only for the briefest of moments, they each felt that something had been taken away from them which they needed in order to be whole.

Then, Percival remembered how the Frenchman had reached through the hat to throttle him, and he realised that, though they had been cursed by the vastness of the years between them, they were blessed to be there, together, in almost the same space.

"Isabelle, my dear Isabelle - may I take your hand?" he asked through his tears, and she laughed through hers and offered him her hand. Percival reached through Time and Space and took her soft, slender hand in his, and her fingers curled around his, and there were no years between them, nor an inch to separate where she ended and he began, and she felt the warmth of his touch envelop her, and her touch in turn radiated through him like early morning sunshine, and they were together.

Then Percival felt the soft breeze brush the hairs on his arm, and realised he could hear the cries of gulls close by, and he could smell the sea! And Isabelle was laughing, and he was laughing, and the world was a riot of colour and sensation, and Percival gripped her hand, so gently placed in his, and asked "My darling, would it be wrong of me to want to kiss you?" and suddenly they each drew the other close, and their two faces met at the brims of two different hats, and they were eye to eye, and they kissed, and in all the worlds and all the times there was nothing, but for that kiss.

"I never want to leave you, my dear Isabelle," Percival declared.

"Nor I you, my darling Percival," an ecstatic Isabelle responded.

"Then we shall find a way. If the world and all the gods in it have brought us together, and have allowed us this kiss, then there *will* be a way. Should we need to move Heaven and Earth and Time itself, we shall do so, and we *shall* be together."

And there, in a dimly-lit dining room on a summer's night in a small English town, and a bright afternoon amongst the dunes on a Cornish bay, two fate-crossed lovers plotted and planned.

There was no way that either could fit through the brims of their hats, of course, and each thought it wise not to try in case the tearing apart of one or both could sever the connection they currently enjoyed.

They committed one another's contact and other personal details to memory, after conspiring in a plan that Isabelle could forward mail or messages across the years, by using a mailing service to deliver mail to him directly at a given time - or perhaps by placing advertisements in a newspaper, for Percival could then use the town's Library to read old, archived copies. In turn, Percival would endeavour to watch the hat at all times, so that, should he encounter somebody who lived in Isabelle's time or before, the same devices could be used to pass on messages to her.

They were delighted with their own inventiveness, and felt as though through their own wits they had outsmarted Fate.

Then, while gazing adoringly into one another's eyes, there was one particular moment in which each of them blinked at the same time, and in that moment the portal disappeared, and the Homburg was once more just a hat, and Percival's room was filled with the shadows of night-time, and yet...

...and yet Percival felt as though he was floating on air, as though he wanted to shout out loud of his love for Isabelle, and the wondrous miracle which had brought them together.

And that, he did. Percival threw open the window to the street and called out to the sleeping town that he, Percival Ray, had met the most beautiful girl, and her name was Isabelle Godwin, and she had captured his heart, and they were in love.

Of course, the response from those residents who had previously been enjoying the comfort of sleep was less than joyful, but Percival didn't care. The world was a beautiful thing, and he was in love.

**

S aturday dawned, bright and wonderful, and Isabelle opened her eyes with a smile. She rolled over quickly, reaching across to her bedside table, and the white lace bonnet atop it.

Alas, on inspecting it, she saw that the bonnet was just a bonnet, a thing of cotton and lace and nothing more. There was no handsome young man inside, uttering the sweetest declarations of love, or making her laugh out loud with the most fanciful of notions. Nevertheless, her heart raced with delicious excitement, and she clutched the bonnet to her bosom, and uttered the tiniest squeal of delight before clapping one hand over her mouth lest she disturb her sister, sleeping in the bed across the room.

Isabelle was, for the first time in all of her eighteen years, in love. Sweet, tender, giggling, laughing explosive love, and with a young man - a very handsome young man, with smooth pale skin and the thickest, coal-black hair - a young man from a lifetime and more in the future, no less! Such a thing was unheard of... and, thought Isabelle, was sure to make *everybody* jealous!

Isabelle sprang from her bed, dancing barefoot around the room in a most libertarian fashion, as though the music of life itself had taken hold of her in some wild, ecstatic possession.

At least, these were the thoughts of Mary, Isabelle's younger sister, who had cocked open one eye while remaining tightly cocooned in the deliciously-warm feather quilt. Mary had often thought her elder - and only - sibling to be something of a wantwit, and a fairy-headed one at that. Her current behaviour only seemed to confirm her suspicions.

"You are a girlish buffoon," Mary informed her sister.

Isabelle, however, remained in splendid spirits. "Oh, Mary, you're awake! Isn't the world beautiful? Isn't the day itself such a wondrous thing of splendour?"

"No," answered Mary, and turned over to resume her horizontal pondering.

Isabelle rushed over to her sister's bed, clambering over her protesting form to lie beside her, despite the younger girl's assertions that she just wanted to sleep.

"But the day is here, Mary! The sun is up, the birds are- can you hear them? They're singing for us!"

"I refer you to my previous statement," came the response. "You are a buffoon."

"No, child, I'm not a buffoon, I'm-"

"Child?" Mary spat, "I'm but a year younger than you, and older by a year or more in sensibility!"

"Perhaps, that may be so," said Isabelle, "but I- oh, do come out from under that awful feathertick, and hear me. I have something to tell you."

"It is *not* a tick, it is a *down duvet*. It is *much* more expensive than a tick, and it is a joy to be wrapped within."

"I don't care!" Isabelle was bursting to tell her sister, somebody, anybody her news. "Mary, sit up and listen." Mary did so, grudgingly, folding her arms before her in protest.

"Okay. The thing is, yesterday, when we were at the dunes, well... I-" For a moment, Isabelle hesitated, nervous and unsure.

"Oh, spit it out, Isabelle," said Mary. "You are truly a girl with cotton in her head."

Then, before Isabelle could say another word, they heard their mother's voice calling them for breakfast. Mary saw her opportunity, and rushed out of the bedroom, yelling "I'm coming, Mother!" leaving Isabelle alone with her fit-to-burst steam-boiler of a secret.

Breakfast was the regular busy affair. Mother had been cooking since before dawn, and the kitchen table was piled with breads and samples of her many preserves. The smells and sounds of bacon and eggs sizzling on the pan filled the large, bright room.

While Mother busied herself at the stove, Father sat at the table, pipe already lit, scouring the print-filled pages of the *Truro Courant*. Mary sat across from him, her mouth already crammed with bread.

Isabelle fair skipped into the kitchen, smiling as she bathed in the bright sunlight streaming through the wide, high windows and the back door, flung open to the breeze.

"Isn't this just the most wonderful of mornings?" she asked everyone and no-one. Mother showed no sign of noticing. Father grunted from behind his broadsheet covering. Mary smiled, albeit sarcastically.

Mother dished out the bacon, and the perfectly-cooked chickens' eggs, set the pan back on the stove, and took her place beside Father at the table. "And what brings you so merry to the table this morning, young lady?" she asked, layering butter on a warm bread roll.

"I..." Isabelle began hurriedly, before suddenly realising her predicament. Of course, she *could* say to Mother "I met a man yesterday while we were at the dunes, a most handsome man, and we kissed, and I spent the night thinking about him, and my dreams were of him, and I woke so deliciously happy because of him, and I think I'm in love!", but what then? Mother would ask "Where did you meet? We saw no young men among the dunes," and Isabelle would have to say - for she could not lie to Mother, on pain of Purgatory - "He appeared in my bonnet, as though it were a tiny window into his world, but it was real, and he held my hand and we kissed, and it was glorious, Mother!"".

Then, Isabelle could see in her mind's eye, Mother's face would darken, and the room would fall into silent shadow as she pointed a finger at her eldest daughter and declared "Begone, foul sorceress! Begone! There shall be no witchery under our roof!", and Isabelle would be flung out into the world, alone and destitute, her face daubed with dirt and her clothes in rags, and people would point and laugh-

"Isabelle? Are you alright?" asked Mother, concern crossing her face.

"I'm fine," said Isabelle. "I'm just happy. It just feels so wonderful to be alive."

"Of course it does, child. Now eat your breakfast before it gets cold."

Isabelle ate her breakfast in silence. Her sister, in the next seat, mumbled through a mouth filled with strips of bacon, "Buffoon."

**

**

For Isabelle, that morning seemed to pass as though in a fog, silent and surreal. She worked her way through her chores as always, helping Mother with the washing of the breakfast plates, the cleaning of the kitchen, and the preparing of the household's laundry for collection - what with Father being a Councilman now, the family possessed the wherewithal to pay a laundrywoman to take care of the actual task of washing their clothes - but in her mind she was torn, betwixt and between, consumed with both joy and torment, for she could scarce hold in the tale of love exploding within her, nor could she express it, for fear she would be called a witch or a madwoman or worse.

Later, when Mother took herself to her bed for her mid-morning kip, Isabelle joined Mary in the yard, where she was idly scattering seed for the chickens. Isabelle took a handful from the sack, and strolled alongside her sister, flicking seeds for the bobbing heads to follow.

After some moments of strained silence, Mary said "Okay, you can tell me."

"Tell you what?" Isabelle responded, with seeming innocence.

"I'm sorry I didn't listen earlier. I just thought you were

being, well, you. You can be a bit of a fairy at times."

"I know." said Isabelle.

"But something really is bothering you, isn't it? Is it a boy?"

Isabelle was still nervous. She didn't want to be cast out as a witch, or forced to live in rags. "I'm not so sure now that I should say."

"Then that's all the more reason why you should tell me. After all, '*a secret kept is a lie told*', or something like that. And also, I heard that keeping secrets can make your hair fall out!"

"No?"

"It's true. I heard it at church. I think. Somewhere, anyway. So tell me - what's disturbing you so?"

"Mary, if I tell you, you must promise to never tell another soul. Not as long as you live, and perhaps not even after that. Do you promise?"

"Really? I-"

"Do you promise?"

Mary promised, making a vaguely-passable attempt at genuflecting, and Mary was too wary a child to break a promise made outdoors in the sight of God. And so Isabelle told her everything, babbling in a rush about the voice in the hat, the face, those beautiful eyes, his lips, his reaching for her hand, their touch, their kiss, oh Lord, their kiss-

"You kissed a boy?" Mary was incredulous.

"Not a boy, Mary, a man! A beautiful man, with kind eyes and soft skin and lips that... and he comes from the future, by a hundred years and more."

Mary stared at her sister for a long moment, and then guffawed. It was not a ladylike laugh, but a loud, full-bellied shriek of delight, that rattled and rolled around, filling the yard. "Oh, Isabelle, you're such a fool!"

And though the laughter was not meant entirely unkindly, Isabelle felt her face flush in embarrassment and anger, and she ran off, out of the yard and along the lane, heading away from the house and the still-echoing laughter.

Later, while sitting on the banks of a happy little stream, Isabelle found the calmness she so sorely needed in which to think properly on her situation. Yes, she was in love, and dizzyingly so. Hence the morning's madness. But she was a grown woman, with a mind to consider a logical and effective course of action, and so she sat in silent contemplation, aided by the stream's thoughtful bubbling accompaniment.

By noon, she had decided on a plan. She would begin to write. She would write letters every day, telling of her life, and of her love for her time-stricken beau, and she would leave out no detail. She would do this for as long as she drew breath, and ask that they be passed down the family line until they could be delivered to Percival in person, to his home in Cornbury in Cambridgeshire in the year nineteen hundred and thirty-nine.

If her plan worked, there was no reason why Percival should not receive her words of love imminently, though not a single one had been written into being as of that moment, and the very thought of it spread a smile wide across her face. And the sun shone down, and the sky was blue, and it was a beautiful day.

When she returned, the kitchen was once again caught in the hubbub of movement and aromas, for Mother spent much of the day cooking in the heart of the home. As she walked in through the open door, Mother asked her to clear the table ready for lunch, as though Isabelle had not been absent for hours.

Isabelle brushed a few scattered crumbs from the table, and picked up Father's paper, ready to place it in the bucket with the kindling at the side of the fire. As she did so, some tiny detail caught her eye in the slightest of glances she had afforded the paper in handling it.

She looked closer, opening up the sheet. Needing more light to make out the fine print, she stood in the doorway to read.

It was near the bottom of the page, just a paragraph, a short message beneath a bold heading, as was the fashion for paid-for advertisements.

The heading read : "*My Darling Isabelle,*" and the paragraph below continued "*We kissed in the dunes, and from that moment my heart has been yours, completely and utterly. I shall love you always, across all of Time and Space, until my very end. Love forever, Percival.*"

And there it was, his declaration of love, in print, against all sense and against all hope. He had found her. And she laughed and she cried and she looked like a madwoman, but she didn't care. And she could see the glimmer of concern in the faces of her mother and sister, but she didn't care. It would all work out. He had found her, and she would write to him, and soon, in one hundred and forty-five years, he would hold her letters of love in his hands, and she will have found him.

It was a most beautiful day.

**

**

That Sunday, Percival woke still filled with delirious happiness, and a smile which had formed before his eyes were fully open.

He'd spent Saturday - at work at the offices of Battersey, Battersey & Kendrick - in a love-bound haze. Luckily, neither Davies nor any of his acolytes had approached him and disturbed his mood, and the taming of numbers was accomplished with a confident flick of a happy man's quill.

But Sunday, O delightful Sunday, his first spent knowing that love was real, and the lips he had kissed had kissed him back, and the sun was shining and the sky was blue...

That morning, Percival took to the street to walk through the soft lovers' breeze. He wore his hat, of course. Now that he knew that at any time it could open a portal to offer him a chance to see Isabelle, or to pass on to her a message, he had not let the Homburg leave his sight. And, as he strode through the streets, he felt a new confidence build inside him. His was the smooth, waltzing stride of a man in love.

There was a festival of some sort happening at Charman Park, in the centre of town, and so Percival headed over, for once feeling as though he were truly part of the crowd. He eased his way through the throng, as the smells of candy floss and toffee apples swept across him, along with the savoury aromas of cooked meats, and there were German sausages - these being a favourite treat for Percival, who had tried one at a Christmas fair one year and had become enamoured with them. One of these, held between two slices of rough bread was, more than ambrosia, the undisputed food of the Gods.

Somewhere out of sight, a fairground organ was playing some of the latest musical compositions from across Europe and the Colonies. Percival found it delightful.

As he stood in the queue for wurst, Percival daydreamed, picturing himself in the same queue but with his arms linked with Isabelle's, that they could both together enjoy the sounds and scents of the fair, and that the world would see them, a young couple in love, and there would be nothing fantastical about it, and-

"Percival!"

With dread immediately gripping him, Percival turned around, to see Davies a few places behind him in the queue. Not merely that, but as soon as he was noticed, Davies began to ease himself forward, apologising, until he stood next to Percival, who suddenly felt himself trapped.

"Percy! My good man. I missed you yesterday - so caught up on things, you know? The way they work us

over at BB's is atrocious, don't you think?" He nudged Percival lightly with his shoulder. "You know what I mean. We're worked like the dogs we are, men like us, Percy. Like damned dogs. So, tell me more about this young chickadee you've been hiding from us. A pretty little thing, is she? I'd wager so. Men like us know how we like our crumpets buttered, right?"

In return, Percival offered a tight-lipped smile and the faintest of nods.

"Of course we do! So, has a name, does she? Your out-of-town belle? Your hidden fancy? Your-"

"Her name is Isabelle," Percival said quickly, in a bid to halt the flow of verbal monstrosities pouring from the loud mouth of the man. "Her name is Isabelle, she is eighteen years old and hails originally from St Ives - that's in Cornwall. She has one sister, named Mary, and-"

"I say, this sounds like the real thing, Percy my man. The real thing indeed. You're sounding like a love-struck pup, which is how we all sound when we've found the One. You lucky, lucky dog."

"The One?" asked Percy.

"Indeed. Does she make your heart spin and your knees collapse? Does she make your lips go weak and your groin burn hot like-"

"Yes. Yes, she does. But I'd rather not talk about..."

"Percy, Percy, Percy. You're among friends. It's absolutely fine. In fact, if you like, I can tell you a tale or two of some rather naughty young things I encountered just last Sunday! Oh, my, but weren't they hungry for-"

"Stop it!" Percival spat. "Davies, you have a foul mouth, and by bringing that to bear in a conversation about my Isabelle, you disrespect her, and I will not have it. So kindly be somewhere else, or... or I shall be forced to punch you."

Davies spluttered for a brief moment, considering a response, but then, seeing the fire in Percival's eyes, thought better of it, and hurried off, mumbling under his breath, shooting back one quick glare as he retreated.

Percival was trembling still as he reached the front of the queue, but he calmed himself enough to collect his wurst and bread, and wandered slowly towards the park's exit. There, he found a bench, and sat to eat, while watching the sun-kissed throng of happy townspeople pass on by.

He was about three-quarters of the way through the delicious wurst when he felt somebody poke his head. The top of his head. From inside his hat.

Percival steeled himself, breathing slowly. He didn't want to bring attention to himself in this public place, but he needed to look inside the hat as quickly as possible in case Isabelle had found her way back to him. He placed the remains of his wurst on the bench, reached up, and pulled his hat down so that only he could see within it.

His heart sank to see that it was not Isabelle's angelic features which greeted him, but those of an elderly gentleman, rather rough-worn, and tired looking.

Despite his sunken heart, Percival remained polite, and introduced himself. "Good morning, sir. My name is Percival Ray. I realise that this is a most unusual occurrence, but please be assured, I am no danger, not a madman nor a practitioner of the dark arts, but merely a man who seems to be in possession of a magical hat."

"Tint naught magickal 'bout it," grumbled the man in a thick, West Country accent. "Just an 'at wi' a man in't."

The man within the hat seemed to sway somewhat, and Percival realised that his latest visitor might actually be drunk.

"Sir," Percival continued, "might I ask where you are right now?"

"Off 'bout Sally Lane," slurred the man, " on m' way to Pig an' spoke."

"Pig and..?"

"Shpoke. Spoke, erm... poke."

"The Pig in the Poke?"

"Aye. You too?"

The man was drunker than a lord, and as intoxicated as he was, he was heading *towards* the tavern. In some frustrated part of his mind, Percival was ranking his hat-based interactions, and the absolute winner of course was the beautiful Isabelle, but he was torn between placing the angry Frenchman and this drunken fool in last place. It was a very close contest.

"Sir, may I enquire as to the year on your side of this hat? I would dearly love to know where it is that you live, and when."

"Why- why would you want t' know 'at?" the man mumbled, his attention already wandering. Percival knew he had to regain his attention.

"I need to get a message to a girl, and if you're in a position to help me, I shall purchase for you a bottle of the finest Rum."

That captured the man's full attention. Suddenly, he seemed a little more sober, somehow. "Rum, you say? Now tha'd be a treat. Th' drink to kill the Devil! What would you need from me, kind sir?" The man almost bowed.

"First, I shall need to know exactly where you live, and

the date."

"Well, I lives at Haroldsgate, a short ride f'm city of Bath, sir. An' it's... I think March, yes, March."

"And the year? Sir, I'll need to know the year."

"Well, it's of th' year seventeen hun'red ninety 'n' three."

Percival was immediately so utterly delighted that he could have kissed the man. He didn't of course, that would have been horrifying for the both of them, but once again for him, the world was bright and filled with Isabelle.

Over the next thirty minutes or so, Percival schooled the man as to his plan. The man - his name, Percival discovered, was Jack Howes, and he was "husband to Martha and father to too many," - seemed to regain most of his faculties as the promise of Rum grew ever more concrete.

Jack was uncomfortable writing an actual love letter to be posted to another woman. He told Percival that it just wouldn't be right - and that should he be discovered, Martha would come at him with the skillet. Again. And so, it was decided that Percival would dictate a message, and Jack would place an advertisement, on a specific day, with a news sheet popular in the area of St Ives. Once their plan was finalised, Percival headed to the stall at the fair selling bottles of whisky, rum and other concoctions, and bought a bottle of *Colonial Brand Rum* for Jack. Throughout it all, he was careful to remember to keep his hand tightly wrapped around the brim of the Homburg, fingers reached well inside Jack's world, in the hope that it should remain, and not vanish too soon.

Once their plan was complete, and payment in the form of one bottle of Rum was passed through the hat, Percival felt himself relax. Jack opened the bottle straight away, of course, and the two men sat, on different sunny days, surrounded by the same air under the same blue sky, one hundred and forty-six years apart, and conversed through the brims of their respective hats as though there was nothing unusual about their situation.

Later, once Jack had gone, and their hats were merely hats once more, Percival wandered idly through the streets of the town, away from the fair. He preferred the chatter of birds to the noises made by the crowds of townsfolk, and he felt as though he could breathe more fully away from the throng.

As he sauntered along the tree-lined avenues, breathing in the myriad scents of summer, Percival daydreamed of Isabelle scouring the pages of local newspapers until she came across the advertisement Jack would have placed. He was sure that it was worded with subtlety, but with enough detail that Isabelle would recognise herself in it. Any passer-by at that moment, if asked to describe Percival's walk, would most definitely have used the word '*jaunty*'.

Wrapped in his own imaginary extrapolation of the events following Isabelle's discovery of his printed declaration of love, Percival did not notice the presence of the uniformed Police officers until he was almost at the front door of his building.

There were three of them there, burly fellows, with a thick beard upon the chin of each.

One of the officers approached him as he headed towards the door of the building. "Mr Percival Ray?"

When Percival answered in a deferent tone "Yes, how may I help?" the officer produced a set of metal cuffs from a pocket.

"Mr Ray, I'm arresting you on suspicion that you did make threats against another person. Now, if you please..." The officer motioned for a stunned and horrified Percival to hold out his hands, and when he did so, placed the cuffs upon them, locking them in place with a small metal key.

A crowd was gathering as Percival was led towards the Police carriage and placed inside it, flanked by two of the burly, bearded fellows, while the third sat with the carriage driver, and the spectators whispered and mumbled and muttered in a concerned, excited murmuration as they devoured the spectacle of the arrest and detention of a seemingly mild man for such a despicable crime.

At the station, an officer led Percival into the detention area, took his fingerprints and requested that he remove his shoes, his belt and his tie. Percival complied, and began to walk towards the cell, where a thick metal door was open, inviting him in.

"And the hat, sir," said the officer.

"I'm sorry?" Percival responded, fearfully.

"The hat, sir." the officer reiterated, with just a hint of impatience. "I will need to take your hat from you before you enter the cell."

Percival could feel his pulse begin to race, and his chest begin to tighten. The thought of his one link to Isabelle being taken from him and stored in a cold stone storeroom out of sight was terrifying. What if she were to reach out to him, only to find silence, and shelves filled with nothing but the secured property of prisoners?

"But why? It is just a hat. Surely it is permitted for a man to retain his headwear while incarcerated?"

"Rules are rules, sir," said the officer, his impatience now clear to the ear.

Percival was terrified. If he had not been quite so fear-stricken, he might not have shouted at the officer. "No! I shall not! Until I am found guilty of any crime, I am a free citizen of the Empire, and as such I demand to retain the dignity of a free citizen, and I insist on asserting my right to keep hold of my hat! It is *my* hat! Mine!"

As the officer stared agog at his obviously hysterical detainee, wondering what on Earth possessed a man that he would react so violently to the loss of a piece of headwear, the Station Sergeant ambled into the detention area.

"What appears to be the problem, Constable?" he asked, in a low, calm voice. The solidly-built Sergeant appeared to be a man with a lifetime of service under his thick, leather belt, and as such seemed to understand that there was a time for barking orders and a time for subtlety, and that this situation required the latter. He stood, thumbs hooked into the side pockets of his tunic, as he awaited a reply.

"I was merely securing the prisoner's possessions for storage, sir," said the Constable.

"Of course, of course," his superior responded, "but surely a hat is no danger to man nor beast? We remove items from prisoners which they might use to harm themselves or others. Is it your opinion that this item falls into such a category?"

"No, sir."

"Then, I'm sure we can allow this man to retain his dignity and his headwear while he remains in our care, no?"

"Yes, sir. Of course, sir," the Constable responded. And with that, the Sergeant ambled on to another part of the station, thumbs still secure in the pockets of his tunic, and the Constable led a grateful Percival to the cell which was to hold him for that evening, until his visit to court the following morning.

"Thank you," Percival said, still somewhat in shock at this latest turn of events. The cold, heavy metal door slammed shut on him with a swift, violent crash. The Constable offered a brief, gruff non-verbal utterance in response as he turned the key in the lock, and then he returned to his desk, leaving Percival alone but for the hat.

A night alone in a cold, stone gaol cell is enough to test the mettle of any sober man, not least one who has not been raised with the expectation that such a night might come upon them at some point in their life, yet through each long, passing moment, Percival was warmed by the rough felt gripped tightly in his hands. But, locked away from the sights, sounds and smells of the world outside, with nothing but the echoes of the distant jangling of keys held on the thick leather belt of the station's wandering Sergeant to break the silence of the cell, Percival felt, for the first time in his twenty-one years, truly, truly alone.

No clock's ticking sounded out the passing of the

minutes, and only the change in light from the small, barred window set high above the steel-framed bed offered a vague accounting of the transformation from evening into night. This was a quiet station, so quiet that Percival wasn't sure whether any other cells were occupied by... by criminals. Those such as himself. For that's what he was now. A criminal. A bad lot. A stain upon the Empire. The thought of his wretchedness clawed at his soul.

Percival's urge was to curl up on the bed, squeeze his eyes tightly closed, and hide from his situation, but on closely inspecting the worn, woollen blanket draped across the disgustingly-stained straw mattress, he decided to fight that urge, and so resigned himself to pacing the confines of the small, cold, stone box in which he found himself.

The box measured five paces, from wall to wall. Not large paces, such as one would employ when walking briskly across the moors, but the restrained paces to be found on crowded pavements across the country.

One. Two. Three. Four. Five. Turn...

One. Two. Three. Four. Five. Turn...

One. Two. Three. Four. Five. Turn...

One. Two. Three. Four. Five. Turn...

One. Two. Three. Four. Five. Turn...

Occasionally, one of the officers would raise the metal flap above the spy-hole in the door, before moving on and doing the same with the rest of the cells. Percival was sure that, on seeing him pacing in the cramped quarters of the cell, the officer would have thought him mad. Cuckoo. Around the bend. Flop-minded. Featherheaded. Bandicoot.

Percival was not quite convinced that this wasn't the case.

At some point during the dark small hours of the morning, Percival - having fallen exhausted onto the rough, filthy mattress and dropped into uncomfortable sleep - heard the sound of voices nearby. They spoke softly, as though not wishing to wake him. He muttered something through his half-sleep, and the voices spoke again.

Percival jumped into wakedness, and looked around for the hat. It lay on the mattress next to where he'd been sleeping, and it glowed with a soft glow like firelight. As Percival picked up the Homburg, he saw why.

The scene within the hat was of a family - a young, bearded man, a young woman who looked to be the man's wife, and a gaggle of wide-eyed children clamped around them, the entire family in awe at seeing a stranger's face before them, peering out from the father's rough felt hat.

Those on each side of the headpieces watched those on the other in silence for the longest time, the only sounds being the gentle crackling of logs on the fire and the distant jangling of keys as the Sergeant made his rounds in some other part of the station.

Eventually, the young man spoke.

"Greetings, friend. You are at the home of Griselda and Herbert. These are our children. Who might you be, stranger?"

"My name is Percival," said Percival. "Percival Ray."

"Welcome, Percival," Herbert responded, his voice a mix of friendliness and curiosity.

"You have a lovely family, Herbert," Percival said. Each of the many young faces smiled. "I apologise if I disturbed your evening. I do hope I didn't snore?"

The chuckling from a number of the children told him the truth.

"My apologies for that also, then."

"May I ask," said Herbert, "why is it that you are here, and how? This is rather unusual. We're not used to such ways, being a simple family. We mean you no offence, and you're most welcome to be here, it's just that..."

"Of course. I completely understand," said Percival. And, from the quiet darkness of the nighttime cell, he told them of his adventures with the hat. The children laughed out loud when he told them of his battle with the angry Frenchman, and Griselda smiled softly when he spoke of finding his one true love in Isabelle.

At one point, Griselda fetched some bread and some warm soup, and they all sat around the open portal together, just like any other family with a guest.

They had been chatting for quite some time before Percival thought to ask. "What year is it there, where you are?"

"It is sixteen hundred and two, and we reside in the county of Devon," Herbert responded.

Percival sighed. "I'm thinking that that is much too early to send a message for the newspaper. I daresay the *Truro Courant*, though it would be closer to you geographically than to me, has probably yet to be printed in your time."

"I'm sorry," said Herbert.

"I'm afraid not even our children will be alive to pass on a message two centuries hence," added Griselda. "Though we can only imagine the lives of the Underbothams at such a time!"

"Underbothams?" asked Percival.

"This is our name," Herbert replied. "It has been such for as long as there have been settlers here at Black Dog."

Percival smiled. "I dare say there are few Underbothams about and around?"

"Few indeed. Our family are close, and not as numerous as some."

"I think I might know of one - from before my time, but after yours," and Percival regaled the family once more, this time with tales of Ernest Underbotham, one of the greatest architects known to the world of the 19th Century. He described to them the magical designs of the walking buildings of Calella, famous still after eighty-some years, and of the Harlequin Hotel, taking pride of place at the centre of his home town.

The family were captivated by these tales of one of their family, known to the world, living in a time far beyond them, spoken of so eloquently by their storytelling guest.

"My dear Percival," said Herbert, "you have given us the greatest possible gift. To know that our family shall not only survive through the years, but thrive in this manner, is beyond any dreams we could have had. And, if it is to be that the Underbothams shall reside here at least until Ernest's time, then surely there will be one of our line who will be suitably placed to relay a message to your beloved Isabelle in her time."

And so it was that plans were made and a message was drafted, and in the quiet hour before dawn, there was merriment in the darkness of a cold prison cell.

**

"*M*y dearest, most handsome and charming Percival," wrote Isabelle, late one evening by candlelight once Mother and Father had retired and Mary had taken to her featherwick and was snoring softly, "*I write once more, that you might know me and the life I live here, in this world so far from your own and yet linked by the love which binds us. And I do love you, my darling man. Though the days pass without you by my side, you are always in my heart, and in my thoughts. Oh, my thoughts...*"

The rough scratching of quill across paper echoed through the stillness of the house as Isabelle poured out her heart, her longings and her passion to her distant love.

It had been three months and more since Isabelle had discovered the note from her beau, hidden in plain sight amongst the trivia of local life printed on the front page of the *Truro Courant*. Amid the notice of the sales of livestock and much dry politicking, Percival's words stood out as though they shone like sunlight, these words just for her, telling of their secret love which broke the bounds of the world itself.

In the time since, Isabelle had written many letters to Percival, keeping them locked away from prying eyes in the chest at the foot of her bed, and the key to the chest hidden away in the drawer of her nightstand.

During those three months and more, however, though Isabelle was wrapped in the dream of a summer's day in the dunes, the world itself had moved on. There was talk of trouble in the Caucasus, and of a third Crimean War - the place had been a hotspot since the 1500s, but since Catherine, Empress of All Russia, had been insulted by some dignitary or other from far-flung parts with strange, unpronounceable names, war was brewing once more.

All of this Isabelle told to Percival, through letters which she fervently hoped would pass through time unscathed. Not a day or night went by without her at some point dreaming of the moment when Percival would receive a package, a bundle of letters of love, bound in ribbon and passed from generation to generation until that day. She would picture his smile, his delight, his laughter and his tears, and it would provoke her to both laughter and tears also, that they had one another and yet were separated by the greatest gulf of all.

Sometimes, in her letters, she would write fantastical tales - imaginings of how their life would be if she were there with him in that strange, futuristic world of his. She would write of strange contraptions, invent new customs and tell of all manner of strangeness which could befall them and yet, they would be together and their love endure.

And always, she would end each letter with new declarations of unending love for Percival, her forever beloved Percival.

One damp, grey morning in the full grip of autumn, Isabelle rose to a house quite alive with activity. She wrapped herself in her woollen night-coat, and headed downstairs to the kitchen to find Mother shuffling from cooker to countertop, as Mary raced to arrange the table as though they were expecting guests of some importance.

"Are we to receive their Majesties?" asked Isabelle. Mother seemed not to notice, nor a somewhat excited Mary. Father grunted his disapproval of Isabelle's disrespect of the Monarchy. He had a talent for saying a lot with a muffled grunt or two.

Finally, her work done and the table looking immaculate, Mary said "We're expecting a gentleman."

"A gentleman?" Isabelle asked, unsure as to what this could mean.

"A suitor!"

"A suitor?"

"Child," said an exhausted Mother from the edge of the

stove's heat, "cease parroting your sister, and go freshen yourself up. He will be here soon."

Isabelle was suddenly gripped with some dread. "Who will be here?" she demanded.

"I told you," replied Mary. "A suitor. For you."

"What?" Isabelle was horrified. "Mother? Father? Will somebody please tell me what is going on?"

"It's time," Mother called over distractedly, her attention held mostly by the new load of bacon sizzling in the pan. "This young man has great prospects, he comes from a good family and is known by your father. At your age, you should be glad of the attention. Now, go and get yourself ready."

"I will not!" exclaimed Isabelle, but nobody paid her any mind, and so she ran back to her room, where she flung herself onto her bed and began to wail.

After some minutes, Isabelle realised that nobody was coming to see what was wrong. Furious, she stormed back downstairs to the kitchen, announcing loudly "I shall not see another man. I have a man with whom I am in love, and he loves me, and we shall be together somehow, one day. I..." but just as quickly as she'd begun, Isabelle ran out of words. Her outburst threatened to cause more problems than it could ever solve, and a small voice inside her told her she should have remained silent, and merely put this young suitor off instead, perhaps by playing dumb, or acting in some childlike manner in his company. Instead, she had possibly placed herself in the middle of a deadly trap, with no way out but the truth, and the truth, she knew, would see her cast out into the world, without family or friends, as-

""What on earth are you talking about child?" uttered Mother, still cooking, oblivious to what had just transpired. "Now please, will you go and prepare yourself to meet this gentleman?"

Father offered another grunt, and Isabelle turned and left the kitchen, still furious, but grateful that her slip had been missed.

Later that morning, the young man arrived. He greeted the family with all due courtesy, and bowed to Isabelle in a most respectful and charming way. It struck Isabelle that, if it were not for Percival, and the strange tale of their love, she would have looked at this young man differently, and perhaps have shown an interest in him, romantically. He was, after all, rather dashing.

The young man's name was Cedric, and, though only twenty years old, he had nevertheless risen to the rank of Captain in the 11th Light Dragoons, having fought bravely and with honour in the brutal Tblisi campaign. Cedric had about him the air of a man who had seen the world unravel, and Death ride abroad. That said, his smile was soft, gentle almost. Despite everything,

Isabelle felt comfortable speaking with him at that crowded family table, and she smiled back.

Mary barely took her adoring eyes off him.

After a period of polite eating, and even more polite conversation, Cedric asked Mother and Father whether he and Isabelle might walk alone in the yard. Suddenly, Isabelle remembered what was happening, and the fear of having to face a suitor's potential advances terrified her. Nevertheless, as both parents happily and eagerly gave their permission, Isabelle found herself nervously accepting Cedric's outstretched hand, and allowed herself to be led by him into the yard, as the rest of the family watched from the kitchen without even bothering to pretend otherwise.

The sky was still somewhat overcast, but it had turned into quite a pleasant day otherwise. It was warm and dry, and occasionally the sun would break through the clouds. As Isabelle and Cedric walked around the yard, close but not touching, chickens darted around them, clamouring for seed.

Isabelle's mind was racing. She had to put this young man off wanting to court her, while remaining polite, and most certainly without giving away the truth, for she did not wish to be seen as a mad girl in the eyes of this friendly, handsome young man. She stumbled over words and half-thought-out sentences, but in the end, as they reached the corner of the yard furthest from the house, it was Cedric who spoke.

"Fear not, young Isabelle," he said. "I've come to you today with a declaration of love, but not on behalf of myself." Cedric's gentle smile matched that within his eyes as, still slowly walking, he discreetly pulled an envelope from within his jacket, and handed it to Isabelle.

"I had not thought that this day would ever come," he continued. "My family have spoken of you for generations, sure that you were merely a story to be told on cold winter nights to warm the hearts of those listening."

Isabelle slid the small, delicate envelope into her dress sleeve, and walked with this stranger, who seemed to have known her for his entire life.

"This letter has been in my family for almost two hundred years," Cedric Underbotham said, before recounting his family's legend of the time when Herbert and Griselda and their young children first encountered the stranger who spoke to them through a hat.

As they walked, and Isabelle listened to the story being told by an incredulous Cedric of how her Percival had reached back into the darkness of time to leave a message for her, she could not stop the tears from running down her face - but on the inside. Inside, where she was leaping for joy, screaming and laughing and dancing, while on the outside she walked calmly, side by side with her make-believe suitor, around an ordinary yard on an ordinary day, with her nervously-excited family watching from beyond the kitchen door.

Cedric left after an appropriate amount of time, and he and Isabelle shared a secret in their smile as he bade them goodbye. The very moment he had left and was out of sight, the family turned to Isabelle, like hungry chickens waiting for scraps. Isabelle merely smiled, told them that she wished to be alone, and dashed up to her bed. There, once she was sure that there were no sororal footsteps following on behind, she ripped the envelope from her sleeve, and tore it open.

"*My darling Isabelle,*" it read. Isabelle almost squealed with delight. She wanted to scream out loud with love and happiness and because she held in her hand a note from her Percival. *Her* Percival. She kissed the paper over and over, before beginning once again, at the most beautiful beginning.

"*My darling Isabelle, my light, my love, my life. Though the years divide us, my heart is yours as yours is mine, and thus our love transcends all that would stand between us, and our words unite us in love eternal. My bonnet-borne angel, my sweet, sweet Isabelle, I send word to you across the centuries, that my love for you is boundless, and will remain in my heart until Heaven itself calls me, and even longer still...*"

Isabelle read on, and though she'd not have thought it possible, fell even more desperately in love with her time-crossed beau.

It was another wonderfully beautiful day.

**

The day was unexpectedly cold. The courtroom was dark and menacing. The judge's decision was offered in a flat and emotionless drone, and his gavel hit the bench with a harsh, ominous crack which echoed like thunder in the grim, grey-painted room.

Percival squinted as he left the court building, his eyes seeking to hide from the cold yellow sun. The judge had sentenced him to pay a fine of ten pounds, after declaring him guilty of *acting in a threatening manner in a public place*, and Percival had somehow thanked the man before leaving his courtroom.

Now, though ten pounds worse off, at least he was free. But what lay behind the wide smile he wore as he made his way home was not the fact that he'd escaped a prison sentence, but that he'd sent a letter to Isabelle, letting her know in as many ways as he could articulate just how deep was his love for her, and telling of his dreams and imaginings, and all the things he could never have placed in a newspaper advertisement.

It was a letter dictated the night before, which would have taken two hundred years to reach her, but would have been read for the first time by his beloved one hundred and forty-five years ago. Percival realised that his life, his love and reality itself were all so spectacularly bizarre, and though he was walking along a public street, with people all around, he laughed hard, as though there was not another person in the world.

When he arrived home, his landlady was waiting for him, as though she knew to the moment when he would return. She handed him some letters and a parcel, which had arrived for him early that morning - "While you were still in prison," she hissed, before informing him that she had no desire to renew his contract of lodging once it lapsed at the end of the summer, and that he would be well-served to find a new place to live, as she wasn't prepared to have *"his type"* living so close to good people.

By the time Percival reached his front door, his mood had shifted from light to dark, and as he slammed the door shut behind him, he cursed the landlady under his breath. He threw the letters and the parcel onto his bed, then threw himself down hard on the mattress next to them, burying his face into the thick duvet covering, and screaming into it.

Later, having calmed himself with some minutes of screaming, raging, and punching the duvet-covered mattress, Percival sat at the table near the window, with a cup of freshly-brewed coffee made from ground beans purchased from the Gibbet some time before, and began to sort through his mail.

Rather unpleasantly, the first letter he opened was a hand-written declaration from his landlady, repeating the same horrible insults she'd offered to his face earlier. He cast that letter aside in disgust, mostly unread, and opened the next.

The next offered no reprieve from the misery which was seemingly being heaped upon him that morning. The dry, typed announcement read simply *"Mr Percival Ray. Please be advised that your presence is no longer required at Battersey, Battersey & Kendrick. Your contract of employment has been voided. Any monies owing will be forwarded to you at the end of this calendar month."*

No *"Thank you for serving us well these past few years,"* or *"We hope you find employment going forward,"* or an offer of a reference. He was just to be discarded, like an old sock which had sprouted a hole.

It was all just too much. "I think I deserve a drink," Percival muttered to himself, and headed back out into the cold, uncaring world so that he might forget his troubles by getting stupidly drunk.

This is something he managed to do rather quickly, for Percival was not a man with a knack for drinking, nor the habit to sustain it without becoming overly-inebriated, especially considering his depressed emotional state. And so it was that, that evening, as a soft breeze accompanied the gentle hubbub of families, couples and crowds passing along the avenues, sitting in the parks and generally enjoying the air, an unemployed and soon-to-be homeless young man could be seen and heard to be acting in a most unsavoury manner.

Rum bottle in hand, Percival sought to commandeer others and drunkenly bark his troubles at them, and appeared to be rather taken aback at their disinterest and disgust as they backed away from him.

"I've lost everything," he slurred, "but I've still got a hat!"

But nobody cared, and Percival slumped onto a park bench, muttering to himself.

The more he drank, the more he slumped, and as the light began to fall from the evening sky, so Percival's world became darker and darker in his mind. He had nothing but Isabelle, and she locked so far away from him that he feared he may never touch her again, and even the kiss they shared seemed to be more imagined than real.

Percival was so lost in his maudlin self-pity, that he didn't feel the tears on his cheeks.

Then, in an instant, his world was rocked with the most devastating blast, which exploded near the top of his head, and threw him from the bench onto the rough tarmacadam of the pathway. His ears rang with a piercing, violent tone, and when he opened his eyes he could see thick, dark blood covering his hands, and dripping from his head.

He looked to his right, and saw the Homburg close by. From it came the most fearsome amount of noise, a terrible crashing, further explosions, and thousands upon thousands of voices screaming. Flashes lit up a scene of hellish carnage beyond the edges of a battered metal helmet, with human bodies scattered across a vista of mud, blood, metal shards and broken bodies, and large, hulking metal machines shooting out fiery destruction in all directions.

Percival reached out and grabbed hold of the hat in his trembling, bloodstained fingers, unable to turn himself away from the sounds of screaming and war, and watched in open-mouthed horror as people died.

After capturing visceral suffering and explosive death for much too much time, the view changed, as someone picked up the helmet from the battlefield mud, and stared back at Percival.

Bright, maddened eyes which screamed of torment stared out from a mud-stained face, barely registering the unusualness of finding a man inside a battered helmet while the world was being torn apart.

"Who are you?" the face shouted, with a voice like the dead.

"My name is Percival," came the shell-shocked response.

"You speak as an Englishman. Do you fight for Britannia, or for the Colonies?"

"I- I didn't realise we were at war," Percival stuttered.

"What? Are you mad, man? We've been at war since April."

"Where are you?"

"Wallingford, Colony of Konektikut. You?"

Percival realised with horror that he was speaking to a man who was fighting during the Konektikut Uprising, and that the terrible violence being played out through the rim of the Homburg was nothing compared to what was to come when, after fighting for five long, torturous years on the trench-ridden muddy battlefields of what was to become the New Haven Free State, the colonials beat down the British forces and starved them to death, refusing to let them leave the mud until every soldier had died, and only then could their bodies be shipped back home - if, indeed, they could be found, which all too many thousands weren't. The horrors those soldiers endured were the stuff of dark legend. Though the fighting ended a few years before Percival was born, he knew the legends from his schooldays, when the boys would sit in silence to hear stories of the valour and heroism of war.

"Cambridgeshire, England," was all that Percival could utter.

"May I ask you a favour, Percival?" the mud-streaked face shouted, raising his voice in part to be heard over the sounds of explosions and screams, but also because by now his hearing was no doubt near-destroyed.

"Of course. Anything."

"Could I ask you to pass on a message to my family? They've heard nothing from me in months, they must be worried for me. Also, I have something." The soldier reached into a pocket, and removed a small, gold-coloured pocket watch. "I don't want these savages to get it. Could you make sure this gets to my people?" he asked, passing the watch through the portal as if this was an everyday transaction.

Percival received the watch without saying a word, and offered a stiff nod in response.

"My name is Deekes," the soldier screamed, the sounds of violence intensifying around him, "Gunner Patrick Deekes, from Upper Barnston in Suffolk. Find my wife Mary, and tell her-"

And there was an abominable sound, a flash of light and a rush of harsh, acrid smoke from within the Homburg.

And then, it was just a hat. Charred a little around the inside of the rim, and stinking of all manner of horrors, but still. Just a hat.

Percival sat for the longest time, in the dark, on the cold, damp ground beside the park bench, oblivious to the world, blood slowly drying on his face, scalp and hands, staring through blinding tears into an empty, silent hat.

**

L ater, Percival made his way home through the quiet, deserted streets, populated at that time only by cats and shadows. After closing his door behind him, he took off his shoes and sat down softly on his bed. Then he lay back, eyes directed towards the ceiling, but without seeing it.

Nothing seemed real. Not even the silence of his bedroom. Not the light entering through the gap in the curtains from the street lights outside, nor the shadows created by it. Instead, Percival's bloodstained retinas pulsed with looped images of the dying and the dead, and his ears replayed for him, unbidden but inescapable, the roar of battlefield fire, and the terrified screams of young men dying.

His eyes were dry, though he hardly noticed. Despite the interminable screams and unending horror, he was empty.

After some indeterminable time, he turned onto his side, curling into a ball, trying to squeeze away the sights and sounds of his brand new madness. As he did so, he rolled onto the parcel which had arrived with his mail, so long ago. He took hold of it, hoping to summon the will to throw it from the bed, when a sliver of street-light glow highlighted the postmark on the creased brown postal wrap.

Truro.

He sat up, wincing with pain, clutching the small parcel in fingers caked with dried blood, scrabbling at the paper, then tearing it when it wouldn't unwrap quickly enough, until the contents spilled out onto the duvet.

Four facsimile copies of the *Truro Courant,* which he'd ordered from the library a lifetime ago and forgotten about, each potentially containing words from his Isabelle.

Percival sat staring at the newspapers for a while, torn between excitement at the thought of reading words sent to him from his love, and the dark, gut-churning horror of the evening which still lay heavy in his belly.

He gathered the strength to raise himself from the bed,

and to head to the bathroom. There, he showered, scrubbing his skin hard in a vain attempt to erase the blood he felt coated him from head to toe.

As though he were in a dream, Percival dressed himself, and then he made a pot of strong coffee to overpower the sickening sensation which filled his insides. Then, he laid the newspapers out on the dining table near the window, and slowly, methodically, began to scan the pages for a sign of hope.

He passed over the main headlines - of trouble in the Caucasus, rumblings of war in Crimea, the death throes of the French Revolutionary Uprising, the sinking of the *Agamemnon* at Naples and the death of her Captain, one Horatio Nelson - and instead scoured the smaller, personal classified advertisements, among notices of births, weddings, deaths and other minutiae of human distraction. And there, in the personal section of the *Truro Courant* dated Friday, the 8th of August, 1794, were the words he needed to salve his soul's deep wounds.

"*My darling Percival,*" they read, "*my life, my heart, my Prince of Time ~ know that my very pulse speaks your name, and always will. Yours, bonded by love everlasting, Isabelle.*"

Percival spoke the words softly as he read them, over and over. He stroked the paper gently, drawing with his fingers a soft outline of words his lover had written for him across an unimaginable ocean of time. *"Bonded by love everlasting"*, she said, and he felt the same, and he wanted to tell her, to let her know how much her words meant to him, and he wanted to hold her, and to kiss her once more. Instead, he kissed the words, and spoke her name to the emptiness of the room.

**

The house was so very quiet, with everybody deeply asleep save for Isabelle, who sat propped up by a mass of pillows in her bed, scratching another missive to Percival. Through the open window nearby, a soft breeze cooled her. From somewhere out beyond the shadows, a fox barked in the night.

"My darling," wrote Isabelle, ignoring the twinge in her wrist from having written so much that evening, yet still having so much to tell her beautiful man, *"the nights continue to draw in, and I do so feel lonely without you as the world becomes darker.*

I mentioned, some pages ago, that Mary is receiving quite the army of suitors, and that in a literal sense at times, as many of the young gentlemen who call are military men, serving over in the East. No doubt your history books will tell you of the horrors of this new trouble in the Caucasus, and the terrible scenes in Crimea, where the people are starving, and yet the country's gold is spent on the ugly abominations of war.

What those books may not tell you, or perhaps cannot, is of the hopeful innocence in the eyes of these happy young men and boys, who in the same moment are as shy as puppies in the presence of my darling sister, tongue-tied as they attempt to woo her, and yet primed to do the most horrible things in the name of protecting the Empire. I'm sure there will be girls such as Mary, young and in love, in the heart of Catherine's Russia, who will see the same innocence on the faces of their own young men, as they too are marched off to fight strangers for a cause they do not understand, nor would have a part in if they were offered a choice.

My love, my mind races faster than my pen in my excitement when I feel as though I'm speaking directly with you. I forgot to mention that only this very morning, I had the most delightful encounter with a Mister Cartwright, a secretary over at the local office of the 'Courant' - I had journeyed there by morning cart in order to place advertisements, announcements of my love for you, to be read of course on a day when time has caught up on the distance between us.

This Mister Cartwright, a stout, rather condescending man, read my penned declarations, and sought to make from them some sort of amusement for himself at my expense. Not only that a young woman should attempt to write, but that she should use such an attempt in order to make a public exhibition of passion and love across an imagined temporal gulf, moved him to patronising silliness.

I must confess that my response was as little thought-out as it was incredibly hilarious, to myself at least.

I informed the boor that I was engaged to be married, and that these words were for my intended husband, who happened to be the Government's Imperial Minister for Temporal Matters, and as such had responsibilities across the Empire in time as well as space. I informed that slack-jawed buffoon that my love was currently touring the reaches of the Empire's future, but that on his return, much would be made of the discourtesy to which I had been subjected.

I was so utterly convincing in the telling of this fantasy that, of course, the man swiftly became obsequiously apologetic, and there were so many muttered apologies for his indiscretions that it was all I could do to keep a straight face until my departure.

Oh, Percival, I so wish you had been there to see such a thing. In fact, not a day goes by that I do not wish for you to be with me, or for I to be with you, that we may share the air of our days. How is it that I can miss you so, when our moments together were so fleeting, if not that this love is meant to be, that we are fated to be together, no matter how impossible that may seem. We two, separated by a lifetime and more, have a destiny to be met which sets us both together, without boundary or impediment. I truly believe this, my darling, and I wait with longing for that day."

As Isabelle wrote on, somehow the breeze from the open window grew warm, as though it were a summer's night instead of one passing quickly into winter, and for a brief moment she imagined that the air from his world had visited hers, and that his time had entwined itself around hers, and she smiled.

**

The next morning, Isabelle woke with a fever. Mary sat close by, mopping her sister's brow with a cold, damp cloth. At the foot of her bed, Isabelle saw Mother and Father standing, clutching onto one another, their faces creased with concern as they stared down at their daughter.

When Isabelle strained to raise herself, Mary shushed her, gently guiding her back down onto the bed.

"Calm yourself, sister," Mary whispered. "Your fever is high."

"I feel fine," Isabelle insisted, before accepting that she had not even the strength to raise a hand to resist. Instead, she lay quietly, allowing her younger sister to tend to her, while all the time her parents stood in silence close by, their faces lined with what appeared to be grief.

"What is it?" Isabelle asked them. "Am I to die? For, truly, I merely feel weak, not drained of life."

"It's not your body they worry for, sister," said Mary.

"Then what? My soul? My mind? I can assure you-"

Mary interrupted her sibling.

"You were ill throughout the night, scaring each of us in turn, gabbling on much as you do usually, but with such strangeness. Speaking of men kissing you through your bonnet, of strange worlds beyond time, and many unknowable things. Mother and Father are worried that the fever might have invaded your mind."

"And you, Mary? What do you think?"

"You are my sister, and I love you," Mary replied, "but in all honesty, I believe..." The younger of the two held her pause, as if contemplating her answer earnestly. "I believe you to be as you always have been - a cotton-headed fairy!"

They laughed, gently, as morning's light softly filled the room. Mother and Father left, muttering apparently satisfied pleasantries, though concern was still etched upon their brows. Isabelle looked up at the face of her younger sister, suddenly seeming older than her years. "I love you, Mary," Isabelle whispered. In return, Mary leaned over and kissed her sister on her warm, damp forehead, and muttered softly, "Buffoon."

The fever passed swiftly, and within a few days, all was

as it was in the days before, and the episode remained unspoken of. However, there was an undercurrent in the home, a discomfort of interrupted glances of concern, which created awkward silences and no little angst all around.

One quiet morning, as Isabelle sat in the yard, flicking stray seeds towards the ever-hungry chickens, Father joined her, sitting alongside her on the rough wooden bench. He sat there for quite some time, flicking seeds in silence. Then, having seemingly composed his thoughts, or having despaired of being able to properly do so, he said "My dear, you should know that if ever you are troubled - by anything - you are really most welcome to speak to Mother, or to myself."

"Thank you, Father," said Isabelle.

"If all truth be told," Father continued, "such... unusual forays of imagination should not be entirely unexpected. You are, after all, a girl... a young woman I should say, who has shown magnificent... creativity of thought, and..."

Seeing her father's helplessness, Isabelle reached over and held one of his large, well-manicured hands in one of hers.

"I'm absolutely fine, Father. There is no reason for your concern. Neither you nor Mother should worry for me. It was nothing but the fever addling and befuddling my mind with pure delirium. I'm sure I have been a testing child over the years, but I can assure you, I am absolutely fine."

"And the stories? Of the gentleman, and the hat, and-"

"Father, I-" For a moment, Isabelle contemplated telling him the truth, but she saw the pain and confusion in his eyes, and that moment passed quickly. "I'm fine."

Isabelle leaned over and kissed her father on the cheek, and squeezed his hand in hers. He, in turn, sighed softly, and his body relaxed somewhat.

"But what if I had told you that it was all true?" she said, the words exploding from her unbidden, but she still with a smile on her face as though the question lacked all seriousness.

Father smiled back in response. "Well, in that case, we would have had to have carted you off to the asylum, young lady!" Then he laughed, and got up from the bench and wandered back into the house, chuckling to himself.

As she watched him step through the door into the kitchen, his laughter trailing behind him as he left, Isabelle determined to never speak of the strangeness of her life again. To be banished and thought a witch would be bad enough, but to be dragged into a dark, wretched asylum by her own father would suffocate her soul to death, and even the imagining of it brought tears to her eyes and a crushing sensation to her heart.

**

That afternoon, a carriage arrived at the yard, bringing unexpected visitors. There were three arrivals - the beautiful, red-haired sisters Ivy, Rose and Victoria Cove, cousins to Isabelle and Mary.

Mother, of course, filled the kitchen with industry from the moment they arrived, delegating to Isabelle and Mary the tasks of settling the cousins, and of ensuring that their every want was met. These tasks the sisters undertook gladly, and with heart. It had been all too long since the cousins had last gathered together, and the ceaseless, excited chatter which soon filled the kitchen was enough to spur Father to offer his mumbled apologies and retire to his study.

Before long, there were cakes, biscuits and sweet treats covering much of the surface of the kitchen table, and those few remaining spaces soon filled with tea poured by Mother into her best china teacups.

The conversation that afternoon, spread out among the six as though forming a bubbling wall of sound, was as bright and animate as the faces of those gathered around the table. First, they caught up on old news, and listed those among the family who had been born, married or

had died since last they had met, with a little gossip on
many thrown in for good measure.

Had the family heard about great-aunty Doris? How she
faced down a bull which had broken loose of its tether
and rampaged through the close streets of Churchtown?
The beast had caused no end of chaos, and no little
destruction, during its short reign of terror, but had come
to a dead halt the moment it encountered the fearless, if
diminutive, figure of great-aunty Doris. Once the
subdued creature had been re-tethered, the grateful
villagers began to celebrate their white-haired hero with
gusto. The festivities drew in revellers from St. Agnes
and 'the Goons', along with the cider-makers of Skinners
Bottom.

Of course, with great-aunty Doris being one hundred and
three years of age, and her not having partied so since the
death of the old King, such merriment was enough to see
her off, and the family buried her not three days later.
The turnout was magnificent, and triggered further
outbreaks of festivities, though these were somewhat less
fatal.

And, of course, they must know the awe-inspiring tale of
the birth of the triplets to cousin Charles and the good
lady Amelia? Such drama there was, to be sure, with
them being delayed so by the most violent storm in the
middle of the Mediterranean Sea, while sailing back on
the *Old Ogmore* following its annual tour of the scorched
and ancient coast of Libya.

Poor Amelia. She most surely should never have joined the tour in the first place, and only did so as she feared their children would be born two thousand miles away from their father, and he of course was there only because he was the Captain of the vessel and therefore rather a required presence.

They had scarcely rounded the Horn of Carthage before passengers began to fall ill, thrust into sickness by means of inadequate cuisine. As they fell, so too did a large proportion of the ship's company, reduced to the unspeakable indignities suffered by all who find themselves sentenced to such a fate.

Cousin Charles did his best to prevent a descent into uncivil barbarity, but he soon realised that he too was falling victim to this damnable plague and, fearing the worst should his beloved Amelia succumb, locked her away in his cabin, separated from all the horrors which roamed the ship's quarters and the sun-roasted deck.

They listed about for three days, as those who had suffered slowly recuperated, and then, when they were ready to once more take full control of both ship and destiny, darkly-humoured Nature set upon them with a most powerful storm, which raged against them all day and night for a further three days. All the while, poor Amelia suffered alone as her pains increased, and her unborn children poised themselves for birth.

It was at the height of the storm, as the wind howled, the

rain lashed and the waves tossed the ship about with terrifying ease, that Amelia's screams cut through the hellish vista, and drew her Captain to her side. And there, in a cabin at the heart of the most violent darkness, Captain Charles Boore and his wife Amelia brought three new lives into the world, and the screams of all three became a cry of victory over the almighty storm.

The way the cousins told the story, the three newborns were the stuff of legend, and it was their defiant cries which drove away the storm, and protected ship, passengers and crew from further disturbance until they arrived, late but alive, at Portsmouth.

Mother, Isabelle and Mary were enthralled by the tales, and enchanted by the telling.

As the afternoon passed into evening and the light softened, to be bolstered by gentle candlelight, the telling continued. All the while, Mother deftly continued her industry - ensuring there was never a space upon the table which was not filled with food or drink, and even finding time to prepare a hearty sandwich for Father, safely ensconced in his study - while still being unbreakably engrossed in the meandering conversations.

Ivy spoke at length of being schooled in Mathematics and History by the fascinating and handsome Mr Lowther, a rugged man from the wildlands of Northumbria. While she spoke of the delights of learning, especially those subjects most often the domain of men, all present understood that her prime delight was the company of *"the fascinating and handsome Mr Lowther, a rugged man from the wildlands of Northumbria."*

Rose regaled her audience with her tales of romance and no little danger, courtesy of her tour of Iberia and the Maghreb. Her beauty inspired suitors from Seville to Marrakech, and her wild nature drew drama and danger to her across two continents. It was said of this nineteen-year-old literal English Rose that she was suffused at the best of times with the gentleness of moonlight, but at the worst of times she raged with the fury of the Saharan sun.

But, while Rose drew gasps of concern, and elicited howls of laughter from those hanging on to her words, it was Victoria, the youngest at eighteen years of age and with the most delicate of tones, who secured their utter devoted attention.

Victoria spoke of her love for a young man - an artist, as free as the wind, and untamed by society - who had passed through the village some months prior, stopping at the inn for a week or so to take advantage of the area's unique light and revitalising air.

The others leaned in closely as Victoria gently recounted the tale of how she first laid eyes on this wonder of God's creation, and how he first caught sight of her, and of how love bloomed in a moment and brought colour to the world as if for the first time. They leaned closer as she described him to them, from the depths of his oak-brown eyes to the taut magnificence of his body. When she told them of how he had held her, and kissed her, they almost slipped from their seats.

There were tears as Victoria whispered how her love had left her, she gazing after him in the early morning light as he walked away from the village and into a different life. She stood, alone, for the longest time, hoping that he would turn around, renouncing his life as a wandering artist to be with her, but his steps, like his body, were firm, confident, and moving away from her forever.

"And what of you, Isabelle?" asked Rose. "Surely you must have a troupe of suitors lining the way for your affections?

The question appeared as if out of nowhere. Isabelle had not been expecting it. If she had, she would not have sat there speechless at the table, her jaw slack and empty of words as the gathered faces all watched for her response. But how could she answer such a question? How she wished to enter into the spirit of the storytelling with the tale of her own fantastical love affair, of her own devoted beau who had traversed time itself to declare his love for her, and yet the trauma of exposure as a witch or a madwoman had sealed her lips, and she had nothing else of interest to offer the expectant audience.

The moment of awkwardness threatened to tear apart the jollity of the evening, and so young Mary took it upon herself to interject.

"There is an encampment nearby, where they train the young soldiers, and more than a few have come to visit - and our Isabelle has been the recipient of the attentions of a Captain, no less!"

And in a moment the awkwardness was forgotten, as Mary soon held the room with her own tales of shy young soldiers and their protestations of love. Mother found her daughter's stories risqué, but hysterically amusing. The house fair rang with the unrestrained laughter of family.

The following morning, the three sisters left to continue their journey towards Bristol, where they would meet with other members of the family and no doubt enthrall them with their entrancing tales of lives lived to the full.

With the house now painfully quiet, Isabelle took to herself, and set off to wander the paths across the common to the north. There was a spot above Hellesveor Cliff where she often went when she needed to think through life's confusing moments - a rock worn smooth from the generations who had come to sit and ponder and found the rock to be the perfect seat upon which to think and gaze out at the endless horizon - and it was to that spot that she headed that morning, with the cousins' tales of adventure still ringing in her ears.

The breeze was light, but with a subtle chill, and the sea calm, and what little spray there was, was carried aloft upon the air, rising to the clifftop, where Isabelle sat watching the shrieking gulls swoop across an otherwise silent vista.

There, high above the boundless body of water which stretched from St Ives north past the tip of Wales to the island of Ireland, west to the settlements of Newfoundland, and south to Tangier, Cape Town and all the way to the pirate coasts off the Bay of Bengal, Isabelle suddenly felt awfully alone.

How she wished, so fervently, that she could see Percival - to sit with him, to be held by him and to speak with him of her woes and her worries. How she wished that she could touch his face, his beautiful face, grazing her fingers softly against the smoothness of his cheek. How she despaired of ever falling deeply into his eyes again.

She allowed the tears to come, fully and without restraint, her body heaving with the pain of loneliness, and the loss of something which had never quite come to be.

After a while, once the pain had subsided into a quiet hollowness, Isabelle began to ponder her life. She was eighteen years of age, and had never had an adventure - save for one, that being her love affair with her time-bending beau, about which she knew she must remain silent, for fear of the punishments that exposure might bring. To her, the world was unknown, and she so dearly wished to know it. And, while her love for her beautiful man still filled every part of her, and delicate strands of hope remained within her that she would see Percival again, she knew that the time had come to walk abroad amongst the world, to be a part of something outside of herself. She knew also that to travel without purpose would be a fruitless endeavour, and as such, she would need to find her own reasons to take the required strides away from all that she had known before, to become something new, to grow and to change.

Such reasons, she decided, should be of use to the world. For, while cousin Rose had delighted all with her tales of passion and danger, her adventures impacted none but herself, and Isabelle wished for her own adventure to be more meaningful; to be something of which she could be proud.

And so it was that, late that afternoon, Isabelle stood in the kitchen of her home, watching fondly as her mother busied herself with preparations for their evening meal, and announced, "I have decided that I must go to war."

**

The coach to Upper Barnston rattled the bones of its few passengers as it was driven along at a furious pace over the rough roads just past the old medieval town of Clare. The widow Sawston had pleaded with the driver to halt for a while on reaching the town, that her body might repair for a few moments from the brutal assault of the carriage's dastardly uncomfortable seating, but the driver had paid her no heed, nor had he seemed to notice the protestations of Percival and the otherwise silent gentleman opposite, as they cried out for respite. Instead, the driver cracked the whip to send both horses into a further frenzy of entirely unnecessary speed.

By the time they reached their destination - the Black Horse Inn at Upper Barnston - all three passengers were cramped, bruised and fatigued from the pain inflicted by both carriage and driver. To add insult to injury, the moment the wounded passengers stepped down from the carriage, the driver raised the whip, and the merciless transport sped off once more in a furious storm of hooves, dust and whipcrack back towards Cambridge, leaving the stunned passengers choking on the dust they left behind. Percival, the widow Sawston and the silent gentleman winced as they limped slowly towards the door of the inn.

While the landlord's wife settled the poor, battered widow, the landlord himself - a relaxed, portly fellow with a cheery disposition and a most impressively wild and full beard which reached almost to the hem of his freshly-washed tunic - escorted the men to their rooms.

The taciturn fellow was offered a most pleasant box room on the first floor, just above the bar, and from there the landlord led Percival up a further rickety flight of stairs leading to the attic.

It was as the two were ascending the steep, narrow staircase that Percival was suddenly soaked with water.

Salt water.

From inside his hat.

Percival found himself caught on the horns of a most horrific dilemma. The landlord was chattering blindly about the village and the people in it to his new temporary tenant, who was only a few steps behind him, but if that tenant began speaking with another fellow who happened to be inside his hat, and the landlord noticed these strange goings on, there would be no telling what would happen. Percival was sure that such things were not usual in this quiet rural backwater of Suffolk.

Also, to add to his trouble, Percival's hands were both occupied with his travelling cases. Any attempt at that moment to reach for the Homburg would no doubt result in some calamity on the narrow stairway.

On the other hand, if Percival were to ignore this new visitor within his headwear, who knew then what could be lost? A chance to pass on a message to Isabelle - in fact, at that very moment, Isabelle herself could be gazing into the hat, wondering why her beau was refusing to answer her call.

In the end, the point was moot, as by the time these thoughts had passed through Percival's mind, the landlord had opened the door to his tenant's room.

"This'll be you, sir," the landlord said, and stepped aside

to allow Percival to enter. Not caring whether it would seem rude, Percival raced past the landlord with some quickly muttered thanks, and closed the door quickly behind him. Only then did he tear off his sopping wet hat, to see who occupied the other side.

There was no angel there, waiting eagerly to catch sight of his face, but instead the bewhiskered visage of a wide-eyed madman, staring back through the rim of the hat with an agitated, crazed look in his sparkling blue eyes.

The skin upon his face was scorched by the sun, pock-marked and blistered something awful, and the wiry growth of dried, bleached facial hair scratched the hat's felt as this stranger brought himself closer.

As the sounds of the landlord's retreating footsteps faded, Percival began to appreciate the sounds breaking through the barrier between their two worlds. The regular crash of waves breaking on a shoreline competed with the cries of gulls, or some similar birdlife, and they in turn fought a strange, unearthly hum.

It took a few moments for Percival to realise that the hum was emanating from the face of this startled, bearded maniac. The hum was tuneless, almost random, yet unceasing, as though it were an accompaniment to the man's breathing.

Percival drew a deep breath, preparing himself for a potential repeat of his disastrous encounter with the vigorous Frenchman. And, yet, within those crazed, hypnotic eyes, something akin to recognition whispered to Percival, as though this were a man he knew.

Each of the men watched the other, silent save for the humming of the hat's new guest.

Then, the stranger spoke.

"Hello there," he said, in a clear, refined and completely sane manner. So clear, refined and sane a manner in fact, broadcast as it was from the face of what appeared to be a wizened Bedlamite, that Percival gasped in shock.

The fellow took no offence. "I completely understand, my good man," was his response. "I can only imagine the shock of confronting my current unkempt visage, and through a worn and stained sailor's cap, no less. Terribly bad form on my part, I'm afraid. I do so earnestly apologise, sir."

Percival stuttered, fell over his own words and began again. "It is I who should apologise," he remarked. "I was caught unawares. Please forgive me."

"Nonsense," said the fellow. "Though I feel introductions are in order." And with that, he thrust one sun-burnt hand through his sailor's cap and beyond the brim of the Homburg.

Percival reached out and gripped the hand, though not

with excessive vigour, as, what with the skin being so markedly abused by the excess of exposure to the sun, he was under the impression that such an endeavour might cause no little pain to the gentleman. "My name is Percival Ray," said Percival.

Unexpectedly, the other man laughed at this. "My, how queer. That is my name also." He saw the shocked look on Percival's face, and added "Oh, no, not entirely so. My first name is Elias. Elias Percival Ray. But rather a rum coincidence, don't you think?"

Percival's mouth dropped open. Suddenly, he saw truly what had been whispering to the quiet part of his mind all the while, since first setting eyes upon this new visitor. "Elias Percival Ray? You are Elias Percival Ray? I - I have your picture upon my wall." Percival realised he was gripping Elias' hand too firmly, and released it. "I'm so sorry, I was just excited, I-"

"Pardon me," Elias said, "but did you say that you have *my* picture hanging upon *your* wall?"

And Percival began to tell the tale, of his meanderings through the Souks of Cornbury, the purchase of a painting of a young man eager for adventure, his discovery that the young man portrayed was in fact his great-grandfather - a revelation which astonished Elias, and drew the conversation off for some time along a familial tangent before returning, of course, to Percival's hat-bound adventures, of crazed foreigners, and the enchanting beauty of the face of love itself.

When Percival was done, a bewildered and fascinated Elias began, at Percival's urging, to tell his own tale.

"I have always sought adventure," began Elias. "From childhood I was considered to be something of a galavant, often to be found astray at some place other than that where I was expected to be. I suspect that, as a child, I must have driven my parents to utter despair at times, for I cared little for my own safety, or for the rules of common sense. Some, no doubt, considered me a wantwit, others to my face declared me a feckless fool. But still, I lived according to my way, and on the day of my seventeenth birthday, having left behind both family and the town of my birth, I signed myself on to the good ship *Pegasus*, she who would follow in the steps of the lost explorers Darwin and Fletcher, to capture and record the fascinating and the undiscovered amongst the flora and fauna of the world. On a bright, clear day in June we set forth upon a flight of adventure into the unknown, south and west to the islands off the coasts of the Americas, and from there, east until the end of the horizon."

Percival was captivated by the telling, while Elias was lost within his own memories. "I learned all too soon that the life of an adventurer was one of danger, deprivation and brutal, back-breaking work. Yet I persevered. Such was the life I had chosen, and once I had discovered the man I wished to become, I worked with some diligence to fit myself to my chosen mould."

"As a lowly boy amongst the crew, yet master of my own destiny, I crossed the tumultuous ocean to São Vicente and the pirate kingdom of Cabo Verde. There, I felt as though I had never lived before, as though every breath I had drawn before entering the tented city of Escondida was a dry, lifeless thing. Whereas I was a child in the world I had known until then, at Escondida I became a man. I learned of the world, of its varied and multi-faceted people, of passion and of fire. During the months we spent at and about the islands, making our home within the tented city, I shed the skin of my old self, and became a new and quite different creature."

"By the time we left, and were headed south to the coastal jungles of Bahia, I was truly at one with my new life, and the man I had become. But, alas, far from land, a man sees his own imperfections, and his own smallness in the vastness of the open ocean. There, at the mercy of all the gods above and below, Man begins to understand that he is nothing but a speck within the cosmos, and this is all it takes to drive too many to madness."

"I shall not dwell on the darkest of days, and the horrors they brought, but suffice to say that, on reaching the supposed sanctuary of dry land, the time we spent in the jungle was less of a mission of exploration and learning, and more of a battle to overcome hunger, madness and cannibalism. Those of us who made it back on board the *Pegasus*, and out once more into the open ocean, considered ourselves lucky to be alive, and made a promise before Poseidon himself to never mention the horrors of those days to another soul. Of course, I tell you this only because I consider *our* situation to be somewhat of a loophole in the agreement."

"Of course," Percival agreed.

"Alas again, and alas. No sooner were we safe from the broken remnants of what once were men and shipmates, than the heart of a storm's darkness tossed us into a new world of merciless torture, and we were cursed to be beaten down by the winds and the rain, assaulted by the roiling sea and thrust through the worst horrors the ocean could create, until at last we were dropped, battered and bloody, into the most terrifying of places for seamen to find themselves."

Percival gripped the brim of the Homburg tightly, his knuckles whitening as he silently urged the storyteller to continue this terrible tale.

"After all that which had befallen us, we had escaped the fury of the sea to be cast into its most devastating state - the empty desert of a calm ocean. There, there was no wind, and the sea was as glass, with not a ripple to be seen. We few survivors surveyed our predicament with mounting unease, save for those older souls who had known such a desert before, and they wailed in fear as though they were infants, unashamed to be seen as such in the face of the merciless, unmoving sea."

"My friend, you should know that there is nothing which will convince a man of his utter powerlessness than to be stranded in the heart of a boundless ocean atop a windless sea. We drifted, perhaps a thousand leagues from land in any direction, baked by the sun during the days and chilled to freezing through the inhospitable nights. Days passed, as did the weeks, and in the faraway homes that once we knew, the seasons changed. As the months moved on, though the stillness faded and the sea became alive once more, by then we were but shells of men, dessicated carcasses drifting hopelessly beneath the sun-cursed deck."

"I do not know how long it was before the day I woke to some unreal stillness, different from before, as though the world itself had stopped turning. I summoned what little strength I still possessed, and crawled up from the galley to the deck and the open sky. Through dry, crusted eyes I saw the shoreline, and realised that the ship had finally encountered land, and run aground."

"I was the only one of the ship's company left alive. All others had either leapt into the ocean, screaming, or faded away like a whisper in the wind. Why I had survived, I knew not. I was certain only of one thing, which was that this gift of life must not be squandered. And so, though I quickly ascertained that this island was but a tiny oasis at the heart of an oceanic desert, and that rescue was perhaps as childish a dream as hope itself, I was determined that I should live, and live to the best of my abilities, to live indeed with gusto."

"And so, my friend, my tale is done. You have encountered me living with gusto in my new home, using my hat to scoop up creatures from the rock pools for supper. How it is that we meet in such a manner is unfathomable to me, but I am indebted to you for your wonderful company."

"How long have you been... on the island?" asked Percival.

"Hard to say," answered Elias. "The seasons are barely perceptible here, but I would hazard a guess and say that I have been alone for perhaps three years and some months."

Percival thought this absolutely horrid, and told Elias so, but the shipwrecked mariner laughed loudly in response. "Percival, my good man, you have no reason to worry for me, for you have saved me from all disquietude and fret."

"How so?" Percival asked.

"You saved me when you told me that I was your great-grandfather, and that you are my descendant. But for this to be so, I should first become a father to one or more, and as this has yet to happen, I can only assume that there shall come a time when I shall be rescued, and with faculties sufficient to woo a woman to be my wife and bear my children. So, you see, until such a time as I sire offspring, I shall consider myself immortal, untouchable by the ghastly hand of fate. I may tarry here for a while or more, but the day already sits in wait for me when I shall move on, and return once more to the land of the living. You are my saviour, sir, and for that I shall be eternally grateful."

Percival smiled, and in doing so he realised that his cheeks were wet, and that he had been crying openly while his ancestor spoke. He apologised, and wiped his cheeks dry.

Elias once more reached through his faded blue sailor's cap to clasp Percival's hand in his. "I am glad we met, Percival, and have had the opportunity to share the wonder of our different lives with one another. I can only hope that, as my day of salvation is prepared for me, that yours also waits for you, that you should be reunited with your Isabelle, and that your love will flourish."

And Percival so wanted to tell Elias how much it had meant to him to have met this man who would sire the line which led to him, and to know of the fascinating adventure of his life, but in one brief moment, as two men separated by 85 years of time blinked as one, a veil was drawn once more between the two, and each was left holding a hat.

Just a hat.

**

**

The sprawling village of Upper Barnston, settled initially by the family of 'Righteous' Lord Barnston within the Royal Forest at Ickworth, was a quaint, almost timeless, quintessential English village. The majority of the several hundred houses lining the packed-earth roads which snaked between the ancient oaks and stately yew trees were historical buildings, time-weathered examples of the best of medieval architecture. Those which had been erected more recently, in order to accommodate the gentle expansion of the local family tree, were built of the same locally-available materials, and to the same exacting standards as those held by those first architects and craftsmen. The resulting aesthetic was one of enduring harmony and beauty.

Percival walked the winding streets of the village, astounded by the differences between Upper Barnston and Cornbury. Whereas his dwelling places, and those of all the people he'd known, had always been regular examples of many in a style, boxes in fact - comfortable boxes to be sure, but boxes nonetheless, identical to their neighbours and inseparable from one another save for such minute details as the pattern of the curtains hung in the parlour, or the colour of the street-adjacent door - each hand-crafted home in Upper Barnston was a unique bespoke creation, with many telling details, from floorplans to fixtures, which evoked the special relationship which had developed over time between each home and the family which grew within it.

As Percival dallied along the way, struck by the simple beauty of exquisitely dappled shade upon the pounded earth pathways and the wild growths of greensward at their edges, his longing mind lured him into an imagining of a life where he and Isabelle, his sweet, sweet Isabelle, would find themselves living in such a place, raising a family beneath the spread of ancient arboreal arms, and laughing just for the joy of it, and growing old and grey until they lay together beneath the rich, fertile earth, remembered for forever by those who would come after, and by the shared marble stone which would tell their story to the world.

The air was sweeter that morning, in that dreamlike place, than he had ever known. Percival breathed the air in deeply, savoured its deliciousness, and as he let the breath slip from his lungs, he felt himself relax. Despite all which might plague him, and indeed despite the unfortunateness which clouded much of the world, it really was a beautiful day.

The Deekes residence was on the outskirts of the village, a burly-built wood-framed home with somewhat of a lean to give it character, its walls painted in full-bodied, dark 'Suffolk Pink'. It was capped with a rough mop of thatch, which looked as though it was in need of some care and attention, but would be enough to keep out the worst of the weather.

From a distance, the house looked as impressive as any Percival had seen, but the closer he came to the varnished dark wooden door, hitched to the frame with thick, iron hinges, the more signs there were that life had been hard for this particular home. In places, the paint had faded or been scuffed away, and there were areas where the daub plaster itself had fallen from the thin wooden slats which had held it. Paint peeled from the wooden frames which supported unwashed, unhappy window panes.

Percival rapped on the door with the heavy iron knocker, and stood back.

The woman who answered his knock, a life-worn, harassed young woman possibly no more than a few years or so older than Percival, was not what he had expected - if, indeed, he had expected anything. It was not her look which caused him some consternation, for she wore the pinafore and headscarf which was the uniform of choice for mothers and housewives around the country. Nor was it her features, betraying as they did her current and possibly ongoing embattled state, which made him belatedly reconsider his decision to venture to this place to fulfil the wishes of a long-dead man. It was, perhaps, that he found it difficult to match the image in his mind of the battlefield-scarred young man, surrounded by muck, bullets and death and dreaming of a home away from war, with that of the chaotic vista which had opened itself to him. Beyond the distracted figure of the homemaker, a scrabble of children bickered and fought around a kitchen table filled with chaos, and Percival's eyes were drawn to the dust and the grime and the wear of the home's dark interior.

With every swift-passing moment, Percival could feel the woman's irritation growing, and so he blurted out "Mrs Deekes? Mrs Mary Deekes?" and as he spoke he knew that the question was aimed more at himself than the figure before him.

The woman gave a grunt, turned and shouted out "Mum! Door!" before heading back into the kitchen, and to the battles being fought there.

Mrs Mary Deekes was a quiet, petite woman, who held herself with poise, despite the tales of sadness and woe which were all too visible behind her warm blue eyes. Grey hairs were swiftly overtaking what once would have been a mane of furious red, but she wore them with pride, unashamed of the passing of days. Percival found her to be rather beautiful.

Mary Deekes led Percival through into a snug, a quiet place away from the unholy noises of rambunctious youth. Once he was seated, she padded away, to return soon afterwards with a tray bearing a teapot and two cups. Percival watched in silence as she poured for them both, and waited for her to settle, which she did with a sigh.

"Mrs Deekes, I really am so sorry to disturb you," Percival began.

"Nonsense, young man," came her response, "I'm more than glad of the distraction. It's not too often we receive guests here."

"Well, thank you anyway," said Percival, with a smile.

"So, what brings you to Upper Barnston?" asked Mrs Deekes.

"I came to bring you something," said Percival, and with that he reached into his pocket, and pulled out a small parcel, wrapped in sturdy brown wax paper and rough twine. "I apologise for not wrapping it with more care, but such things have never come easily to me. I'm afraid that if I tried I would make a most abominable mess, and this thing deserves more, much more than I could provide."

Mrs Deekes took the offered package gently from Percival's outstretched hand, and turned it over in hers.

"What is it?" she asked, before slowly beginning the task of unwrapping the parcel.

Percival had pondered his response with some gravity, for he would have so wanted the widow Deekes to have had some clarity as to the nature of her husband's passing, an honest retelling of events so that she might not feel as though his final moments were so distant from her as to be in another world, and yet, if he were to proffer a story of having met the young Gunner only recently, via the mechanism of a hat which had allowed them to converse as though the years between did not exist, he was sure that the woman would think him a fool at best, and a charlatan at worst. And so, doing what he thought was best, Percival told her that the watch had been reclaimed from his father's property when he had died recently.

"My father rarely spoke of those days," Percival said, "I'm sure they were too painful for him to revisit, let alone re-tell. But, I remember on occasion, when the mood was wont to take him, when he would speak briefly of friends and allies left behind in that place. One of these, a young Gunner named Patrick Deekes who, on facing his end, had passed this watch on to my father with the expressed intent that it be delivered to his beloved Mary. Unfortunately, the aftermath of that war meant that my father was never able to travel again, and remained at home with us until his passing. It was only later, as my siblings and I were exploring our father's possessions, that we came across the watch, and I remembered the promise he had once made. I'm sorry it has taken so long, and I can but hope that it brings you some comfort to hold in your hands that which your husband meant for you."

He'd hoped, imagined, that she would smile, though she might have one small tear in the corner of one eye, and perhaps thank him for having delivered to her a piece of her husband, so long gone, taken from her in a war so far away, and there would be some light in her life once more, though tinged somewhat with years-old grief, but instead Percival endured a most deep and uncomfortable silence as the once-young Mrs Deekes sat sobbing without making a sound, her fist clenched around the timepiece.

For the longest time she sat, shoulders twitching to the beat of swallowed pain. All the time, the screams of boisterous siblings and the agitated retorts of their mother permeated the thick stone walls.

Eventually, the silence ended, and the sobbing was once more re-absorbed by the widow Deekes.

"Thank you, for this," she said. "I apologise for my response, but..." she sought out the words for a time, and sighed. "I never wanted him to go. It was a senseless war, created by a few evil men with the aim of filling their coffers to overflowing with gold. It was never about people, only money and power. And I knew - we all knew - that those who would benefit would never be those who fought. Such men would sit back in their finery, drinking port together as those who earned them fortunes died alone, and in Hell. But my Pat, he wanted so much to be able to offer more for his family, to have his children be able to take more advantage of life than he'd ever been able to. I told him that all we wanted was for him to be here, to tend the gardens and to hold his children, but..."

Once again, she sought words, and found only a sigh. Percival realised that he could offer nothing in return, and for a long while the silence remained.

"Life is nothing without love. I'll tell you that, young man. Nothing. But, had I known that my love would desert us to follow a path without return, I would honestly never have loved so in the first place. I would sooner have harboured the loneliness of a spinster all of these years than the dessicated emptiness of a widow. Such things as love perplexed are sure to tear apart one's soul."

"But surely, love is all," answered Percival, shocked at the woman's response. "Surely, if one might know love, even for a moment, one is made the greater for it, and life has more meaning?"

There was a coldness in the woman's voice as she said "To know one moment of love, and to spend a lifetime yearning for its return, removes all meaning from life, and life without meaning is merely a prelude to death."

Without warning, she held out the watch, turning her face away from him. "Take it, and go."

Percival was eager to refuse, both the watch and her icily-uttered premise, but the stony certainty of her demand crushed his impulse. Baffled and frustrated, he took the watch and, uttering whispered apologies, he departed the Deekes' home, leaving behind him the widow's silence and the children's manic cacophony. He strode away swiftly, not caring for direction or destination, intent merely on the act of removing himself from that place, and from the words which rang loudly in his ears.

As he walked in dappled beauty on a warm, summer's day along the softly meandering paths, an unexpected rage bubbled up inside him. How dare she? How dare she disrespect love, and call into question its place at the centre of life? By what right did she impugn the name of that which caused all things to be, and to need to be? Love, even unfulfilled, was the breath which brought forth life from the clay. Where some might imagine gods to have created all things, Percival was resolute that all things were created by love, and through love continued to be.

As Percival passed by the outer parts of the village, striding beyond the old, crumbling boundary wall, he thought of that which love had brought him, and which had breathed life into him. Love, personified, was his Isabelle. She was his air, his sustenance, his *raison d'être*. Though time conspired against them, to keep apart that which had been joined by love, and though the road to reconciliation was cast about with thorns and other bedevilments, he would sooner die than to disavow their love. Though he would give all that a man might give in order to gaze upon her for one more moment, he would lose all things also to keep alive those few precious moments they had enjoyed together. Love, Percival declared to himself and to the world, transcended all things. Love was eternal, and no defeated widow's curse would convince him otherwise.

Having walked off his unexpected rage, Percival stopped at the side of a small stream, and sat for a while to catch his breath and calm his heartbeat to a more acceptable tempo.

As he sat, perched on the bank among the wild grasses, listening to the sounds of the country day, Percival pondered whether all lives were as queer as his. "Surely not," his befuddled mind said to itself. "For other men appear to be occupied with the most banal things in life, and devoted to mediocrity over adventure."

"But of course," said another part of his internal theatre, "you are privy to only the visible signs of a man's existence. Should you become, through some machination, witness to his inner dealings, to those adventures which stride forth from the heart of a man without being visible to the world, you should perhaps have a different understanding of him."

"I hear and respect your wise opinion," came the response from within, "but I'm of the opinion that were a larger coterie of individuals to be embroiled in such an unusual state of affairs as I, then this world would be rife with the bizarre and the unexplained."

"And is it not?"

Percival offered an internal stutter. On considering the matter, he was forced to admit that yes, the world was indeed rife with the bizarre and the unexplained. Even those pieces of the world he had seen or learned about were packed silly with the bizarre, and even a matter as simple as that of the creation of a flower was so opaque as to be utterly unexplained, and unexplainable.

"Touché," Percival replied, out loud.

After a while, Percival sensed that the day was becoming unexpectedly warmer. He decided that he should not rest by the stream for much longer, but instead make his way back to the Black Horse Inn, and pack his cases in preparation for his return home to Cornbury the following day.

It was at that moment that he felt a familiar tap, on the top of his head.

On removing his hat, and gazing into the world within it, Percival soon realised that it was not the day in Upper Barnston which was warming up, but that a new world had encroached upon the Suffolk day. For, within the Homburg, staring calmly back at him, was the blackest man Percival had ever seen, and beyond him stretched a wide, unspoiled vista of golden hues reaching back to a most distant horizon, upon which hovered a spectacularly giant sun, perched magnificently beyond the man's shoulder.

Dotted across the land was an astounding assortment of creatures, a multifarious menagerie of wonder. Many were of the kind Percival had seen in his schoolbooks, and in the showings of natural films at the cinema - elephants, gazelle and wildebeest, dark-eyed vultures and calm, sturdy buffalo. A dazzle of zebras were congregated around a small pool, seemingly relaxed, but no doubt alert for any predator which might sneak its way across the wide, open grassland. Other creatures were unknown to Percival, and some of those he found to be strange and not a little unnerving.

At the heart of this captivating vista was the beaming black face of his latest visitor, staring back at him as though investigating Percival's world with the same sense of wonder.

Percival had never seen such a black man. He had encountered brown-skinned people from across the continents when they had passed through Cornbury, usually heading upwards from the ports at London towards the sprawling markets and spires of Cambridge itself. The Empire was filled with a wide array of peoples, different from one another in size, shape and colour, but Percival had never seen a man *so* black. It was as though his body glowed a deep, deep blue, like the sky in the moment before the true darkness of night. In contrast, his eyes were bright, and alive with a softness which was disarming considering the unusual situation in which each man found himself.

"My name is Percival," said Percival, and he smiled.

The other man, on seeing Percival's smile, stretched back his lips in a wide grin, allowing a great, white-toothed smile to erupt from his face. When he spoke, it was with a deep, rich tone which totally entranced Percival, though he didn't have a single clue as to what his visitor was saying.

Upon realising that each man's tongue was indecipherable to the other, Percival laughed out loud, and the other fellow followed his cue and issued a most heartwarming bellow which echoed across the golden savannah spread out across his world as well as the hearty green of Percival's Suffolk surroundings.

The two spent a good while together that afternoon. Though the lack of a shared spoken language was a hurdle to adequate communication, they soon found that they had no need for it. Each passed their hats around their own world, showing the other the wonder of that particular place at that particular time. They spoke softly to one another merely to exchange the different sounds of their languages, and laughed together as though only they two existed. Their true conversation was spoken with their eyes and their hearts, as each man truly saw the other before them. Percival was glad that, before their bond was broken, he had the opportunity to grasp the other's hand, and each of them spoke unknowable words of friendship across unknown barriers of space and time, until there was in each world just a man, holding a piece of headwear, smiling.

**

The journey back from Upper Barnston to the interchange at Six Mile Bottom was remarkably less violent than that unholy trek which had bruised Percival so only two days prior. He was the carriage's sole passenger, and the journey was thankfully peaceful, and without incident.

The hamlet known to locals solely as '*Six Mile*' was built for the most part around the interchange at the Green Man Inn, set alongside the crossroads which offered passage in all directions, to Cambridge, London, to the northern counties and right across to the far-flung reaches of Dorset and Cornwall. Here, carriages converged, horses were fed and watered, and passengers took a while to stretch their legs, eat a warm meal, and perhaps rest overnight from a long journey.

It was still not yet lunchtime when Percival arrived at the interchange. He did indeed take time to stretch his legs, though this was more for the sake of it than through any need, having had such a comfortable ride from Upper Barnston. As he wandered the dusty grounds of the inn, busy with transport and the shuffling of people, he took a moment to gaze out at the narrow, straight roads heading off to all four corners of the compass, and he pondered on the comings and goings of so many lives, carried from towns and cities across the country to pass through this small, unpretentious gathering of families devoted for the main part to caring for those strangers who, in most cases, would never return. He pondered, too, on the strange and peculiar series of events which had led him from his days spent surrounded by numbers and people in the offices of Battersey, Battersey & Kendrick, to this place from which people had set off in all directions, towards places and lives each filled with their own kind of wonder.

Percival told himself that such a place had no doubt served as the starting point for many an adventure, and by a most magical coincidence, it was as that thought skated across his mind that he caught sight of a carriage preparing to board its passengers and set off on such an adventure, and he heard the carriage driver call out "All passengers for Penzance."

And Percival knew instantly what he was about to do.

**

**

"*My* darling Percival*,*" wrote Isabelle, sat one night in the semi-silence of a hospital ward, "*it feels as though it has been a lifetime since I've had a chance to write to you, and too many lifetimes since we met, and kissed and fell in love. So much has happened that I can barely keep a hold upon that which I've experienced and that which I've hoped for. There are times, my darling, when I feel as though I may perhaps be quite mad.*

Since last I wrote, I have moved into town, and am lodging at the home of my cousin Clara, and her wonderful family. Though I miss Mother and Father, and even my annoying little sister rather hellishly, it is a wonderful experience to be so free, at liberty to pass to and fro at my own convenience. My aunt and uncle are rather strict, of course, but they are rarely present, both being rather busy with either business or society or both. As such, Clara and I have the most delicious time together, as we are well-suited in our humour and our zest for living. She is as much a fairy-headed girl as I, yet amply more brave, and of indomitable spirit.

This is, of course, a rather rapid and grand change in my circumstances, but it is not without its reason. You see, my darling, it was your love for me which not only inspired me, but gave me the confidence to act upon my inspiration. Without you, I should have no doubt fallen prey to my parents' wants, and married some suitor or another, settling with him to offer children and a home life while burying my own dreams deeply within myself, never to be known to the world. But, because of you, I realised that my dreams were worthy, and that if a man as wonderful as you can pledge his love for me across the years which hide us from one another, and in doing so light a fire within me which burns brightly and shall not be ignored, then it would be remiss of me to continue to hide from the world that which makes me the woman that I am.

I have realised that I have much to offer to the world, my darling, and that I might be of use to those who have not been blessed with the wonder of such a love as that which inspires and drives me. As such, I have taken the decision to train as a nurse, that I might care for the wounded and the dying across the battlefields of the Crimea, where war is being fought upon the streets and fields, and our men and boys are suffering and dying in terrible number, no matter what lies spew forth from the lying men of Parliament. I have been here, at the infirmary at Barnoon Hill, some weeks, and have tended to many men who suffer the most outrageous of injuries, both of the body and the mind. So when the newspapers tell their readers that no such horrors are yet being suffered, I feel no discomfort at labelling them liars and snakes.

I apologise for including such harshness in my letter to

you, but I have made a promise to myself that I shall recount the days of my life, that one day those of mine who live on into your time might hand them to you, and that my words will speak of all that I have seen and done and hoped for across the bounds of my life. Though it is my sore wish that we should meet again, to touch again between our worlds, should it be that I die without kissing you one more time I shall still end my days happily with the memory of our first, most beautiful kiss among the dunes.

I continue to purchase the 'Courant' when I can, but alas, their pages are empty without your words. I'm sure that it cannot be easy to find ways to send word backwards a century and more before your own birth, but hope still burns within me. If nothing else, my sweet, sweet man, you have made of me a purchaser of newspapers, and what a delight it is to see the faces of the shopkeepers when this girl enters and hands over her pennies for such things. Even in the town, it is quite the thing.

It is quiet here on the ward tonight. It is one of the rare nights when men sleep. Perhaps it is the full moon which comforts them with its light, but for tonight there is no screaming, no explosions of fear as they are cast out from bloody, terrible dreams. Tonight, there is peace. It is on nights like this that I ponder the days ahead. For it is true, my love, that I have made my decision with open eyes, yet however I still feel no little trepidation, that my days might perhaps end in some foreign field at the hands of some unknown and perhaps unknowable enemy, and worse, that my family may proceed with their lives for some time, quite unaware that mine has ceased. It can be a scary, lonely feeling.

But I shall not end on such a downcast note, dear Percival. Instead, I shall end with a jest which was passed on to me only yesterday, and caused me to laugh out loud in the very ward where I was tending to one unfortunate young man's bed pan. I was most perturbed, as Matron was then still continuing her rounds, and my red-facedness in turn caused much laughter amongst the patients. Nevertheless, I shall tell of it, in the hope that you will see that my humour survives even in a place such as this.

And so. A beggar sat at the gates of a great university, asking for alms, declaring to all and sundry that he was a poor scholar. A learned gentleman, on being approached, did respond to the beggar in Latin. The beggar shook his head, and declared "Good sir, I must confess that I am at a loss."

"But dear fellow," replied the gentleman, "did you not say that you were a poor scholar?"

"I did," replied the other, "a very poor scholar indeed, as I understand not one word of Latin."

I do hope this raises a smile for you, my darling, as much as it entertained the raucous company of the ward, though I'm sure I shall have to deal at some point with the wrath of Matron who, I'm afraid, suffers somewhat from a deficiency of humour.

I send you my love, as always, and kiss this note in lieu of your lips, until it is held in your soft hands, to touch where my lips have been.

Yours, in love until the end of all time and beyond,

Isabelle.

**

The journey from Six Mile Bottom to Penzance was to take four days. Having purchased a ticket on impulse, Percival had been excited to have set forth upon an adventure, travelling across the country on a whim, and he thought once more of Elias, and wondered whether he would ever discover his great-grandfather's fate.

The first day's journey had been more uncomfortable than he had envisaged, but only because so many hours of the day were spent racing violently upon rough tarmacadam or ploughing slowly along muddy, unpaved roads in torrential rain. For some reason, summer had turned its face away from the travellers, and instead they had fought the cold and wet at every turn.

Percival had travelled with three others in the close

confines of the carriage, and despite the inevitable unpleasantness which apparently forms a great part of travelling for those who spend some time packed into a small space with others - not least the odours of those who have perhaps been travelling for some time, and without adequate facilities necessary for their own personal care - Percival was nevertheless pleased that the day had passed without any hat-based disturbances. Such a thing had played on his mind during those moments between suffering the hazards of cold and wet, and the silent onslaught of bodily secretions.

Yet, he had survived that first day, and was safely - and warmly and dryly - situated in a bunk at the King's Head Inn at Blandford Regis, on the outskirts of Oxford. Across the room, Mr Sykes was snoring. A fellow-passenger on the long journey to Penzance, Mr Sykes was an amiable, if somewhat intellectually-impaired young fellow heading back home across country, having suffered the failure of his bookselling business on account of enjoying the company of other heavy drinkers rather too much.

Apart from the irregular eruptions of the room's sleeping resident, the inn was a quiet place. Percival lay on his bunk, unable to sleep, listening to the distant sounds of the night-time wildlife in the fields surrounding the inn.

The first day's journey may have worn him out physically, but his mind clear sped with excitement at the thought of the adventure ahead, and of his final destination.

It had rushed upon him in an instant, upon hearing the call for passengers to Penzance, that this was his chance to breathe the same air as his Isabelle, to eye the same features in the landscape, and walk the same roads upon which she travelled in her time. He knew that if he made it to St Ives, he would become closer to her, and perhaps, perchance, if they were closer geographically, the Homburg would deign to offer them a tryst right there, and they could sit together, upon the same bench overlooking the bay, and such a thing as magic would exist.

With thoughts of Isabelle wrapped around him, Percival finally slept.

Early the following morning, all four passengers were once more shoehorned into the carriage, their baggage strapped to the roof and the sides, and the driver cracked the whip, setting them off once more towards another day of rattling monotony.

The kitchen at the King's Head had provided each of the passengers with a packed lunch for the journey, which was a godsend, as they'd left just after dawn and there was nowhere else open in the village at that time from which they could purchase sustenance. By eight o'clock, each of the passengers had already begun to tuck in to their lunch.

Mr Sykes had devoured the corned beef sandwiches before Blandford Regis had passed over the horizon behind them, and soon afterwards began chomping noisily on the thick, shortbread biscuits.

The two other passengers - Miss Daisy Pickering and her mother, Mrs Pickering, had averted their eyes as Mr Sykes had begun to stuff his sandwiches into his mouth, grunting with pleasure as he did so, but eventually the moment arrived when they gingerly opened their wrapped packages, and sought to daintily nibble at the coarse bread provided. Each kept a free hand placed before their mouths. They may have been eating in public, but they weren't heathens.

Percival had followed Mr Sykes, though with a little more finesse to his dining manners. He at least wiped the crumbs from his shirt after eating, unlike the uncouth young gentleman who, on completing his very early lunch, simply rested his head upon his chest, and within mere minutes was snoring softly, as though he were a child atop a goose feather mattress.

Mrs Pickering shot Percival an accusing look, as though the snoring were somehow his fault, perhaps by the simple virtue of him also being a man. Percival ignored her, and stared out of the window as the countryside passed them by.

They travelled on in this way for a while, and easily so, as they had reached a part of the road which was recently laid, and smooth to ride. The young Mr Sykes continued his rhythmic annoyance, and the ladies Pickering sat opposite, suitably composed and in silence.

And then.

Percival was used to being prodded on the top of his head by that time, but when he felt a warm hand caressing his scalp, he froze. As he did so, some muscle must have twitched in his face, for he attracted the attentions of both ladies. Though he wanted to dissuade them from staring in his direction, he found himself staring wildly back at them, causing more curiosity, and more staring. All the while, a hand was fondling the top of his head, around his hairline, almost reaching out with strange fingertips to touch his ears.

Percival suppressed a cry of consternation, but it found its way out from between his tightly clamped lips. The ladies stared with increased intent, and growing suspicion, and even the slovenly Mr Sykes seemed as though he may soon stir from his slumber.

And the hand within his hat began to grab roughly at him, until there was no more he could take, and Percival ripped the hat from his head and pulled its open interior close to his face - suddenly finding that his face was mere inches away from that of the same furious Frenchman he had encountered so long ago.

Percival screamed loudly, and the Frenchman shouted

abuse - of course, it was in French, but it sounded as though it was abuse, or worse. Mindless now of the presence of other passengers, caught up as he was in fear and confusion, Percival continued to scream at the contorted face within the confines of the Homburg, his hands gripping the brim as though he were strangling this foul invader. In response, the Frenchman did the same thing he did on the first occasion of their meeting, and reached through their combined hats to grab Percival by the throat.

Percival felt the rough fingers curl around his exposed throat and grip it tightly. He felt the blood pound in his head. He felt himself screaming before he heard it, but there it was, a scream of a desperate man -

- waking up in a carriage to find two concerned ladies and one amused young man staring at him. Percival looked around at them, then quickly checked the hat. No Frenchman. No grasping, choking fingers. Just a dream.

Of course, Percival quickly apologised, and the Ladies Pickering brushed off the event as nothing, as did Mr Sykes, but with a smile of no small amusement hooked at the corner of his mouth. After that, Percival spent the day staring out of the window, his hat gripped tightly in both hands.

The rest of the journey passed without incident, though the occasion of the nightmare-driven eruption remained a source of deep embarrassment for Percival, and he knew that it rested at the forefront of the minds of the other passengers all the way to Penzance. Percival was only too happy to debark as soon as the coach pulled up at the Royal Barn at the edge of town, two full days later. He grabbed his cases and fled, sure that he could hear the humiliating sound of young Mr Sykes' laughter as he departed.

Not an hour later, the horrendous events of the journey had faded, and Percival was riding an easy cart from Penzance to St Ives. Before sunset, he would arrive at the town that his Isabelle called home, and be surrounded by things and places which reminded him of her, and he would feel safe, at last.

**

My darling, Percival, how I long to see your face, to hear your soft voice telling me that you love me so. It is at times such as these when I need you most of all, for the memory of you has been my sustenance and my strength for so long now, and yet the world moves forward, dragging me with it into darker and darker days.

My love, the war draws ever closer. Our men and boys are facing Catherine's vicious hordes nose to nose, and there has been sorrow visited upon almost every home in England. What terrible, terrible days we are witness to, that 'war' should be a word known to all children who should be gaily at play. Terrible days, indeed.

My days are spent attending to those poor things who have suffered so at the hands of the enemy in that distant land, all too far from home. Such horrors they have endured both at war and through the journey back to welcoming shores. My nights are slim reprieve from the terrible things I have seen, for they, and worse, are replayed across my dreams, and more and more, sleep eludes me.

And yet, despite my discomfort in the dark hours, I have been unable to shake off the notion that there is a purpose to my life which has so far eluded me; a reason, indeed, for my existence.

My love, I pray that you shall understand what drives me to do what it is I must, albeit strange enough to tell you of it in a letter which shall not be read for a century and more beyond today. It is enough to make me smile somewhat even during the darkest of days here, that our love, and indeed our life together, is so unusual as to almost be farcical, and would most probably be so if we hadn't fallen so deeply in love on that warm day among the dunes.

Our love is the bright, shining light within my life, and the distance which separates us is for the most part an unholy thing which I curse daily, and yet, as the days here draw darker and more full of woe, that distance is also the shield which protects you from the horrors here, for I would not wish for you to suffer them purely for my sake.

I am at a loss to describe the confounding upset within my thoughts caused by our star-crossed love.

And yet, I am meandering some distance from my point. Such is the state of my mind at this moment in time.

My love, I have completed my training as a nurse, and I have chosen to accompany the next caravan to the Crimea, that we might bolster the number of nurses upon the battlefields there, and treat the men and boys as they are hurt, rather than wait until they have endured the journey back to England, by which time a good many of them usually die, or are left as close to death as can be, making the work of the doctors impossible.

I have spoken with the Matron, and my request has been accepted. I depart in a week or so, and the journey will take a good few weeks, perhaps a couple of months if we fall prey to the cold, the rain or the war.

I want you to know, my darling Percival, that I do this with a full understanding of the dangers I might encounter, and the full measure of the consequences should the war fall directly in my path. I hope that you can be proud of me.

I will continue to write, as much as I am able. I only wish I could see your face as you read my words.

Oh and of course, such a cotton-headed fairy am I, that I totally forgot to mention that you have set the town afire with such gossip. The whisper is abroad throughout the streets and the parlours that a secret love affair is being carried out in full view of the town. Of course, this delights me much, though I cannot say aloud that these most delicious and heartfelt poems which have been appearing in the pages of the Courant are directed at me. But they are, my most wonderful man. And I adore them. I have enjoyed them twice over, for the love you have further declared, and for the exquisite jollity of seeing a town so perplexed by a mysterious passion broadcast loudly and yet with silent voice. You are an incredible man, my darling, and to you I send all the love that I possess, through ink on pages to be passed on through the years which stand as the barrier between us. Together we are proof that such a barrier is not impermeable as stone, but instead is as the air, through which our lives and our love all pass.

Be well, my love. I send this note along with long, secret kisses.

Isabelle.

**

**

Percival sat at a table outside the Sloop Tea Rooms, overlooking the grand vista of the Harbour Sands. He was troubled. The coffee in the cup before him had cooled, undrunk, and the beauty of the day passed him by, unseen.

He had arrived at the Stagecoach Inn two weeks prior, just as the sun was setting over Porthmeor Bay - a few streets to the North of Harbour Sands - drenching the world in red and gold. Apart from the face of his love, Percival had never seen anything so beautiful in his entire life. Before even considering venturing towards the inn to deposit his cases, he'd stood, watching, as a miraculously large fiery orb settled slowly beneath the watery horizon, turning the sea to fire as it sank. Though he was not a religious man, Percival had felt something beyond himself in the magic of that sunset, something which seemed to soothe the very heart of him, and in that moment he had taken it as a sign that all was well, and that he was exactly where he needed to be.

His room at the inn was sparsely decorated, but warm, and homely. During the two weeks he had spent there so far, he had slept soundly, the gentle to and fro of the tide along the shore assuming the role of a rockaby lullaby. When not sleeping as though he were an infant once more, Percival had spent his time walking the rambling, cobbled streets.

He found St Ives to be a rather pleasant little town. The locals were quick to offer a nod, and a warm greeting, and just as happy to leave a man to wander the streets wrapped in his own thoughts. The local dining was far from the refined delicateness of the restaurants of Cornbury and Cambridge, but was nevertheless a fresh and hearty delight, with a most surprising range of assorted sea foods whipped from sea to plate by knowing hands at each step, and cooked to delicious perfection.

All the while, his thoughts were of Isabelle. While he sat on the cobbled terrace overlooking one bay or another, he pictured her there, staring out at the same horizon, sitting on the same stone bench, smelling the same salty air. When his fingers reached out to touch the wood frame or the stone of a building he knew to have been there in her day, he wondered whether she had touched them too.

He felt so, so close to her, and yet...

He was torn, and the pain he felt as a result was physical, and growing more dire by the hour. For, the closer he felt himself drawn to the reality of her life, the more he was reminded of the distance between them. The more he saw of the world which would have surrounded her, the closer he felt to her, and the more the lack of her presence cut deeply into his soul.

He could not stop loving her, nor would he ever wish to,

but what purpose that love when time stood as an insurmountable barrier between them? Were his remaining days to be comprised of long hours waiting for a perplexed visitor to arrive at the hat, his heart racing in expectation that he should see the soft, perfect features of his beloved once more, to hold her hand in his, her eyes in his, and to kiss her once more, and if not her then at least to receive a guest who would be of assistance in passing on word of his love by one mechanism or another? Was he destined to be forever but one tiny step and a million long miles from his heart's desire? Surely, love was never meant to be so cruel?

And what of Isabelle? Her days, long since passed, had yet to be lived, and a life spent waiting and wanting would indeed be hellish for her also.

But what if there was a way for their love to thrive? If there was a chance, even one so infinitesimal that it might be missed by the naked eye, then surely that chance for such a love as theirs must be seized and fought for?

Percival felt his thoughts rush about his mind in terrible circles, unable to escape into the open waters of clarity but instead caught in rapid eddies of confusion and angst.

As he sat, pondering the ruthless vagaries of fate, an old fellow came up to the table, pulled up a chair and sat down next to Percival. He slumped into the chair with a soft sigh, and remained there, neither looking at Percival nor acknowledging him in any way. Percival returned the favour, and both men sat in silence, eyes drowning in the distant, sea-soaked horizon.

After some time had passed, the man spoke, unbidden, and apropos of nothing.

"There are monsters in the water," he said.

And then, for no apparent reason, and quite unexpectedly, Percival said "I have a time portal in my hat."

"Sometimes I see them, like dark lights swimming beneath the surface at night," was the man's response.

"I've fallen in love with a most beautiful young woman, though she lives a century and more in the past," Percival declared.

"Sometimes, I think perhaps I might swim out to them," said the man.

They continued to sit, each close enough to reach out and touch the other, but not doing so, instead facing out towards the sea, neither acknowledging the other by way of word or look, as though each were speaking into the wind.

"I love her deeply, but I fear I may lose my soul if I cannot be with her."

"We are taught that monsters are terrible creatures, but what if they are just different kinds of people?"

"I came here to be closer to her, but the closer I've come, the further she seems from me."

"I think I could love a monster. The question is, really, could a monster love me?"

"I've never been more lonely, or more lost. My employer has discarded me, and soon I will be forced to leave my home, and yet I am consumed more fully with the pain of heartbreak and despair."

"My own family could not love me, and have indeed piled misery on me, and yet they are seen as pillars of this community, while those who swim freely beneath the waves are to be considered unholy creatures. I think perhaps the world has been turned upside down."

"I think perhaps I have been cursed with a most beautiful thing."

"I will go to them tonight. I will slip into the water, and swim down towards their light. Then, at least, I shall know."

Then, the man stood up, his face changed somehow, as though infused with a calm determination, and he quietly walked away. Percival continued to stare out at the infinite horizon, and no small part of him was envious of a man who had found the courage within himself to face the darkness of uncertainty with such easy acceptance.

Percival decided to remain in the town for a while, to spend his days seeking out something of the essence of Isabelle. He walked out past the town's border to the quiet lanes and open fields beyond, and for some time he sat and watched the comings and goings of the family who lived in the house which was once the place his love called home. He'd hoped that it would bring him some kind of enlightenment, but instead he felt shame in his furtiveness, and he left that place. Another time, he found himself walking through the rows of headstones at the cemetery, torn between wanting to see proof that Isabelle was real, to see something of her life encapsulated in eternal stone, and dreading to come across a permanent and final testimony to her unquestionable death.

One day, he received a visitor through the hat, and for a while he felt somewhat raised in spirits. The gentleman was a merchant, living in London in 1795. He was not thrown by the unusual interaction as, he told Percival, "I have seen much on my travels across the Empire, from the mysteries of the sadhus of India to the magic of the fakirs of the Levant. A gentleman in my topper I consider par for the course."

Percival spoke with the visitor of his plight, and the gentleman was more than delighted to play a part in facilitating a courtship which seemed to defy all convention. Percival passed him some short poems he'd written, further declarations of love, wrapped in verse as a disguise to all but Isabelle, and the man promised that he would place them in the '*Courant*' gladly, and without delay. Then, in the blink of an eye, the hat was empty once more, and the day seemed a little colder, though the sun shone still, and the world continued to turn as though oblivious to Percival's aching heart.

Late one evening, as the town lay hidden beneath a moonless sky, Percival walked down to the water's edge, looking out across the unending blackness, wishing he could catch sight of the lights below the surface, and envying the man who could.

**

One cold grey morning, with the drizzle sheeting across the dock, the Troop of the Sisters of Barnoon Hill set sail from Plymouth aboard the ageing, creaking *Charon*, headed across the agitated waters to the old port at Saint-Malo. Isabelle sat amongst her fellow Sisters, huddled together on the lower deck to escape the weather, and barely offered a backwards glance through the stained, brass-rimmed portholes as the land which had borne her faded from view.

She had made a good many friends during her time spent in training, and she had become somewhat of a maternal figure to many of the Sisters, even though some of them surpassed her in years. She had been told often that the

Sisters were taken with her gentle ways, and with her composure even when faced with the results of the horrors to which the men they cared for had been subjected.

Isabelle had pondered this with a wry smile as the oak-timbered *Charon* lurched across the choppy waters into the unknown, wondering what her younger sibling, the vivacious and worldly-wise Mary, would think of her fairy-headed sister so grown, caring for others with calm sensibility.

And so the first stage of their journey, though wracked with the ceaseless swells of a tormented sea, passed without much unforeseen drama. Those among the Sisters who became unwell were tended by others who did not themselves suffer the unfortunate agonies of sea-sickness.

Upon their arrival in France, the Sisters were placed under the protection of the King's Favour Dragoon Guards. These were men who would not venture to the battlefield, but instead were sworn to escort and protect the men, equipment and supplies sent by the King across land and sea to where the fight was to be had. In times gone by, they had served in Palestine and Persia, and in times before that had been credited with safeguarding the caravans laden with manpower and supplies along the entirety of the Western Silk Road, from Constantinople to the Khyber Pass, thus ensuring the victory of the King's army over the Maharajas of Rajasthan.

Isabelle found them to be rather a surly lot.

Their passage across the French landscape was eerily surreal. It seemed as though the entire country was in silent mourning. There was no gaiety, no singing or laughter to be heard from the open flatlands of Basse-Normandie to the vast ancient forests which covered Lorraine. The silence continued to haunt them even until the tree-cloaked valleys of the Alsace, as the caravan passed through village after village populated by gaunt-faced villagers with blank-eyed stares. When one of the Sisters asked why the people were silent so, they were told that a deathly fear was abroad in the streets and avenues of France, from the Strait of Dover to the Mediterranean Sea, following the brutal suppression of the recent attempted uprising. The King had shown no mercy to those who would foment rebellion and revolution in his realm, and the peasants had suffered horribly as they were fed not with bread but with the sharpened steel of sabres and bayonets. Worse still, those towns and villages found to have been in league with the rebels had seen their children snatched from their arms, taken from them by Louis' soldiers, never to be seen or heard from since. Such was the terror and despair of the peasants of that sorry Kingdom.

The fourscore of wagons which made up the caravan made slow progress across France, avoiding as they did the major towns and cities - for fear of violence at the hands of undisciplined units of the King's army who might ignore the Dragoons' notes of passage, or indeed, at the hands of savage, bomb-wielding Communards - and favouring instead the muddy backroads where only the threat of random banditry loomed large.

In a forest clearing one evening, not long before the caravan would pass from France into the violence-plagued Prussian Lowlands - a scattered patchwork of competing tribal areas which formed the Western border of the Habsburg Empire - Isabelle sat with a number of the other Sisters as they ate. Their gentle chatter, subdued as it was, hung about in the air along with the free-floating embers from the fire. In the distance, the lower tones of soldiers gathered in quiet conversation could be heard.

"Do you not fear anything, Sister?" asked a fresh-faced young woman of Isabelle.

"I'm sorry?" Isabelle responded, her reverie broken by the unexpected question.

"Pardon me," the young woman continued, "but I have watched you for a while now, as we sit in these dangerous parts, surrounded by shadows which could hold the worst of things, and we on our way to the unholy terrors of war, and yet often I see you sat as though this is naught but a spring day along the coast, where there is nothing more of which to be frightened than a stray gust of wind which might seize one's hat. And I see you smile. Why is that?"

Isabelle laughed, an unexpectedly loud and yet charmingly infectious laugh. "Oh, dear me - Alice, isn't it?"

"Yes ma'am," answered Alice.

"Alice, I would sooner be swept into the freezing ocean at the heart of a raging winter's storm than be torn from my hat, of that you can be assured!"

And Alice and some of the others laughed with Isabelle, though they were unsure as to why they did so.

"Then you must be in possession of a most extraordinary hat?" said Alice.

Isabelle smiled as she pictured her white lace bonnet, the very one through which she had met her Percival, it being now tucked safely away in a discreet pocket in her coat - for she dared not travel without it, lest her time-parted lover should reach out to her and she be far away in some foreign land, and a beautiful tryst might be unjustly thwarted. "Indeed," she answered after some moments, "for it is my link to the one person, in this world or any other, who holds my heart in his most perfect hands."

The Sisters gathered round, and though some had heard this love story before, they too leaned in as Isabelle began to recount her great tale of love, passion and insurmountable obstacles. Of course, she was not so feeble-minded as to allow the exposure of the real truth, and so instead of speaking of a lover whom she had met inside her hat and loved across the divide of a century and more, she span a tale of how she had fallen deeply in love with a sailing man, he not often in port, and of a boundless love torn apart by time and by the sailor's mistress - the infinite, all-powerful sea.

The women were entranced with the storytelling, such that the peril of their circumstance faded into the soft night-time shadows, and their eyes shone in the glow of the firelight.

Later, when the fire had mellowed, and most of the company were asleep, Isabelle sat with Alice, enjoying the peacefulness of the pre-dawn forest silence. They huddled together against the slight chill of the night, and stared at the soft-glowing embers dancing in the fire pit.

"Sister," said Alice, her eyes still locked on the warm glow before them, "do you not ever think that perhaps your life would be easier if only you were to choose a man who was... more present?"

"You mean, rather than a man whom I barely see, and with whom I cannot share the tiniest facts of my day face to face of an evening?"

"Exactly."

"The honest answer to that, Sister, is yes. My life would be much easier."

"Then..."

"Why?" Isabelle sought an honest answer. "Because there was never a choice. I did not choose to fall in love with Percival. My heart did not request my permission to beat so upon seeing his face, nor my soul to delight so when we kissed. Some things are beyond our control, and perhaps beyond our understanding. In fact, I doubt there is much within the world as opaque and unknowable as love, and all of its workings. We cannot hope to understand it, we dare not fight it, and without it we are mere shells of people, walking through our days as though we are real whereas, in truth, life only becomes real when it meets love."

For a while, Alice said nothing, but instead was quietly thoughtful, and then she said, almost in a whisper, "I think I may want to fall in love." And the two women sat together, wrapped in the night, far from home, and pondered the timeless fancies of love.

**

Percival was captivated by the sound of the gulls. Their confident cries woke him in the mornings, and filled the clear skies through until nightfall. They were omnipresent, guardians of the heavens, looking down on mere Humanity as one might look down on an insect grubbing through the dirt with some unknowable purpose. Some days he would spend hours sitting on one of the old stone benches which littered the seafront, his eyes closed, his heart soaring alongside these swooping, gliding owners of the air, majestic, wild and free. Of course, he was bound in time to open his eyes, and to know himself for the earthbound creature that he was, and curse himself for it.

Being in the town was no longer a joy. Every moment served as a reminder that his Isabelle was no longer there, nor anywhere. It had been almost two weeks since he'd last discovered his hat populated by someone other than himself, and he was finding himself to be at a loss. He'd explored the town, with its local beaches and overgrown, secluded pathways which navigated the coastline, but the link he'd hoped for - a much-craved sense of connection to his beloved Isabelle - did not manifest. No matter how many times he traversed the streets of the place she called home, or how often he breathed in lungfuls of the same fresh sea air that she would have breathed, he did not find himself closer to her. In fact, contrarily, perhaps ironically, the longer he remained in the town, the more he could feel her slipping away from him, and the idea that one day he might wake and not be able to visualise her face, or remember the sweet scent of her breath, caused his heart to beat violently in his chest with the terrifying fear of such an awful thing.

One bright, blue-skied afternoon, as Percival meandered blankly along the cobbled streets, filled as ever with the same babbling crowds as the day before, where the same calls echoed across the same market stalls as familiar faces continued to ply their wares, Percival's feet came to a halt at the doorway of a rather run-down stone building in the south of the town, near to the old coach house. The cobbles in the short side-street were rougher there than elsewhere in the town, and the place bore an air of weariness and neglect. The grime-coated windows offered little clue as to what lay beyond them, but a small, hand-written card posted near the door was vaguely legible. Percival leaned forward and squinted to read the words written on the card.

"Apologies," it read, "but the museum has been closed for the foreseeable future, owing to damage sustained in the recent fire. We apologise for any inconvenience." It was signed by "D.G. Maynard, Curator," and dated the 12th of June, 1923.

As Percival stood there, leaned over and peering intently at the sign, the door's lock rattled, and the door itself was pulled open. The tiniest old lady Percival had ever seen barely stifled a yelp of surprise, clapping one delicate, finely-wrinkled hand over her mouth for a moment before removing it to utter "Oh my!"

Percival took a step backwards. "My apologies, ma'am. I was passing, and found myself here. I was merely reading the sign-"

The old lady shushed the visitor at her door, stepping back inside before motioning him to enter. "Of course, of course," she said, with a voice so childlike that it was at first disconcerting to hear it come from this grey-haired, fae-boned apparition. "Please, come in," she added, and much to Percival's confusion, he stepped through the doorway without hesitation, as though his feet, and the rest of him no doubt, were under her spell.

As he stood there, in a small room filled from floor to ceiling with a most diverse collection of artefacts, ephemera and unfathomable things, he felt instantly, and curiously, at peace. It was as though his body had known where it needed to be, and had led him to the exact spot - where, perplexingly, someone was waiting who was not in the least surprised by his presence at her door.

Percival continued to ponder his most unusual current situation while the old lady busied herself shooing dust from random assembled items, all the time chattering with her childlike voice.

"The dust has rather accumulated, I'm afraid. But then, what's to be done? There will always be dust, and where else should it be stored but upon the things? Of course, it wasn't so before the fire, but then we had others come to help, didn't we? And people. Visitors. They would come, and the dust had barely time to settle before new ones arrived, stirring up the air. But now, not so much. And so, the dust settles, as dust is prone to do. And these *are* old things, are they not? And so, perhaps, we should expect there to be dust. This isn't some fancy tea shop, with fresh china and polished silverware, is it? No, no indeed. This is a museum, a place for old things. Things which have outlived their owners, and are set out of time. Much like its curator, some might say." She offered a slight, half-chuckle, almost to herself. "Tea?" And she disappeared into a backroom, somewhere behind a pile of something and a stack of other things, leaving Percival alone in the one-roomed repository of items which had outgrown their owners, and their time.

He first explored the room with his eyes, while in the background the clinking of cups and the happy muttering of the old lady documented the ongoing story of the making of the tea.

At first glance, the room seemed merely to be piled high with the detritus of many lives, but on closer inspection Percival ascertained that the room was actually filled with a rather amazing collection of items which, though perhaps not valuable, were telling of their time, and the lives in which they had played some part. This quiet museum of people's things reminded him very much of the rambling shops in the Souks in Cornbury, though this place was somewhat more introverted, more intimate. This was not a place which focused on the selling of objects, but of appreciating them, and Percival thought that perhaps that was why he felt so relaxed.

Carefully, he stepped between the aisles composed of tables, chairs and other furniture, each item piled high with an array of objects. Many were instantly identifiable. An original 'Busby' phonograph, complete with a selection of wax-coated cylinders. A cast iron mangle and a selection of early hot-coal flat-irons. Scythes and other farming hand tools. Other items were less-easily identifiable. Most of them made of wood or cast iron, and some bizarre implement made up of a selection of threaded hagstones set around a large millstone. There were old photographs, of men, women and children, each staring out at a world they had long since left behind.

"Tea?" The strange, tiny, chatterboxing old lady appeared beside him as though from nowhere, quite startling Percival.

"Thank you," he said, taking the cup and saucer from her. He then realised that he had yet to introduce himself. "My apologies. My name is Ray. Percival Ray."

"Yes," said the old lady, and smiled. She stood before him, cup and saucer in hand, looking up at him and smiling.

"And you are..?"

"Oh, my! I'm Dorothy, dear. Dorothy Gladys Maynard. Curator." She placed her cup and saucer on top of a pile of old books, themselves set on a haphazard collection of old wooden wine cases, and held out one delicate hand towards Percival. He took it gently, half-afraid that he might break it if he was not sufficiently careful. "Sixty three years," she continued, apropos of nothing as far as Percival could tell, withdrawing her hand and reaching for the teacup. "Since old Mister Rogers brought me in to assist on Saturdays. Because of the sorting. Mister Rogers would always need a girl or two for the sorting. I mean, things must be in their correct places, mustn't they? What kind of world would we live in if things were incorrectly placed? We'd barely know where we were, would we? Of course, Mister Rogers is gone now, and so have the other girls. It's been me alone for the past I don't know how long. Not much of a call for the place of late. It's a changing world, you see. People are more concerned with what's new than what's been and gone. Such a shame. But ours is not to reason why, is it? As Mister Rogers used to say, there's a time for everything, and everything in its time. One day, people will want to look back again, to see what's been before. Is it okay?"

Percival was confused. "Excuse me?"

"The tea. Is it to your taste? Only, I forgot to ask you how you take it, you see. I'm prone to forgetting these days."

"It's delightful," Percival responded.

"Oh, good," said Dorothy Gladys Maynard, Curator, still smiling.

"A strange question perhaps," said Percival, "but do you happen to keep newspapers here? Old ones?"

"Of course. We have periodicals, magazines, ha'penny

sheets, allsorts from all over. We have local titles and ones from much further afield. Falmouth, Newquay, Truro."

"Truro?" Suddenly, Percival was excited, and just as suddenly, so was Dorothy.

"Yes! Let me show you. We keep them at the back here. Please take this," she said, passing him her cup and saucer. He took them from her, and then looked for a place to place both them and his own crockery down somewhere safe, while Dorothy continued to narrate her endeavours.

"I do so love the newspapers. Tales as old as time, they say, and they're not wrong. People have been doing what people do for the longest time, and I find it heartening to know that as many problems as we have in the world today, there were as many yesterday. People loved, people married, people died and others followed, and such has been the way for all of the ages of Man, and so shall it be until the last day. To see the stories of real people living their lives immortalised in print really warms my cockles - if you'll pardon my language. I'll just take a look behind... the... Here we are. What would you like? Local? Erm, Padstow? We have-"

"Truro?"

"Truro? Yes! Yes, we have..." Dorothy was silent for a moment as she sorted through a selection of printed sheets. "We have the *Courant*?"

"Yes please!" replied Percival, rather too excitedly. Not that Dorothy seemed to notice.

"Year?"

"Well, erm, I don't suppose by any chance you'd happen to have anything from the 1790s?" he asked, quite confident that Dorothy would say no. Dorothy disappeared again below a stack of old papers, sending small dust clouds floating up towards the ceiling.

"Let me... 1790s, 1790s... 1795, 1795, and... yes, 1796. Any good for you?"

It was as much as Percival could do to refrain from snatching the proffered copies of the *Truro Courant* from Dorothy's slight hands.

"You find yourself a place to sit, young man. I'll go and make us a fresh pot of tea." And then Percival was alone, holding newspaper sheets which would have been printed while Isabelle had been in the same time and place, thinking of him while he was a century and more in the future holding those same papers and thinking of her. The twisted humour of time was rather dark, Percival thought.

He perched on the outcrop of a small stool, which bore also a number of trays, stacked atop one another and topped with a selection of silver cutlery. From there, he laid out the first sheet of a *Courant* from February, 1795, across a table crammed with an assortment of items made of the stuff of History, and began to scan the pages, savouring even the words of articles most obviously not concerning Isabelle, and enjoying them as a part of her world.

The typeface was more compact than was found in modern newspapers - utilising a small-sized serif font with a narrow leading - allowing for more words per page while remaining perfectly legible, which Percival thought was rather a shrewd business decision, though it did mean that he had to squint to read some of the more verbose articles.

The main articles illuminated the reader's mind as to the ongoing troubles in the Caucasus and the Crimea, as well as the brutal clampdown on the peasant population in France. There were some rather beautiful sketches featured alongside a glowing report on the ceremonies marking the establishment of the Batavian Republic in the erstwhile Netherlands, with all the good and the great gathered in Amsterdam for the festivities. The lower half of each page was reserved for stories of lesser import, or for advertisements and promotions. Percival scrutinised each parcel of text, hoping for some sign of a message which stood apart from the rest, something which would leap out from the page as an obvious declaration of love across the ages, but nothing sprang from the page for him.

It was while examining the pages of the third copy of the Courant, that Percival had some detail catch his eye enough to cause him to stop, and to read one particular article in depth. The story spoke of the travails of the wounded soldiers returning from the Crimea, and of those who were trusted to nurse them back to rude health.

"The Sisters of the Infirmary at Barnoon Hill are preparing for a most epic trek across the barbarous regions of Europe, stinging still from famine, revolt and revolution, to the vicinity of the battlefields of the Crimea, where they shall work in service to the wounded, and be charged with the respectful burial of our dead," read the article, *"and though their mission be perilous in the extreme, the Sisters are determined to meet such a challenge with true British courage in the face of that most vile scheme of rampant Russian brutality.*

They come from far and wide among the towns and villages of Cornwall and Devon to train at the Infirmary, and do so with such quiet dignity as can only be expected of the good women of England. One such, Miss Isabelle Godwin of Penbeagle, when asked of her fear of war, stated that her fears were only for the continued suffering of those valiant soldiers who fought to protect liberty in the Crimea, and that she was proud to be offered the opportunity to play a part in such a noble cause, and to have a worthwhile meaning made of her life. Such is the bravery of these fine young women, soon to tread the pathways of Europe..."

Percival read the passage again. And then again, his fingers tracing the words as his eyes passed over them. " *One such, Miss Isabelle Godwin of Penbeagle...*" - Isabelle. His Isabelle. Her words there on the paper where they had sat for one hundred and forty four years, as though waiting...

He realised that he was holding his breath, and caught himself before his knees buckled beneath him. If it hadn't been for the corner of the stool, he imagined that he would have keeled over for sure. A subtle cough caught his attention, and he looked up to see Dorothy looking at him with an amused intensity. She still wore her casual smile, and asked "Tea?"

Some time later, Percival sat with Dorothy in a small room behind the museum proper. He was relieved to be able to sit on an actual chair, soft and yielding, rather than have his bones knocked by the hardwood stool. Dorothy sat opposite him, having brewed a fresh pot of tea, and poured them each a cup.

"I could not help but notice that the newspapers had caught your attention," she said.

"More than you could know, thank you," Percival replied. "May I ask, do you know much of the history of this place? I mean, one can only glean so much from an old newspaper article."

"Indeed," said Dorothy, "but if you read them all, you

may find you have a better understanding of the larger picture."

"And have you?"

"Have I what, dear?"

"Read them all?"

"Well, of course. I have been here for quite a while, as I think I mentioned. In fact, I think I must have read every book and newspaper here several times over."

"That's impressive," said Percival. "By any chance, do you remember much of the nurses from the Infirmary?"

"The Sisters from Barnoon Hill?"

"Yes."

"I do indeed. Poor, poor girls."

In one brief moment, across the course of two short sentences, Percival experienced hope that he would hear some more tales of the Sisters, and perhaps even of Isabelle herself, and then felt a crushing fear at the pity in Dorothy's tone.

"What happened?" he asked.

"They never came back, you know? Not a one of them."

**

Percival stumbled blindly through the rain, the wind-driven drops adding cruelly to the stinging wetness made by his tears. As his feet slid across the soaked cobbles, almost unaware of the harshness of the evening's weather, he bellowed as though he were a beast in pain - which, in fact, he was.

The tale which he had heard from the quiet-voiced Dorothy Gladys Maynard, Curator of a ghost of a museum, had torn his very soul in two. For, it was a tale in which, though unwittingly, Dorothy had told Percival of an unalterable truth regarding the one object of his love and deepest, most heartfelt affection.

The Sisters from Barnoon Hill, she had told him, had left England for the battlefields of the Crimea, and had indeed intended to assist the wounded and the desperate there, but instead found themselves setting up an infirmary at a camp somewhat short of the battlefields themselves. During one terrible night, their infirmary - along with the surrounding barracks housing upwards of a thousand weary fighting men and boys - was attacked and over-run by soldiers of Catherine's unstoppable army. "They were barbarians," Dorothy had told him, "sparing none, and acting out the foulest abominations of war."

Percival had heard the words as though they were spoken in some undecipherable tongue, as if spoken in some unknown dialect of ancient, impervious Sanskrit, as his mind battled to refute their existence in order to best protect his sanity - for, if a grain of truth were to exist within the foulness of those spoken sentences, then all was lost, and in such horrific fashion.

Percival had covered his ears as Dorothy's words continued their assault upon him. He'd leapt to his feet and rushed from the tiny, one-roomed museum, careering about it and causing the remnants of lives and times gone by to tumble and crash and clatter to the floor as he made his way out, through the door and onto the street.

The world, and the wind, whipped by him; lashed and tore at his anguished torso as he raced through the uncaring night and howled into the sky.

At some point, unnoticed by this wounded beast which trudged the rain-soaked cobbles, evening gave way to night, and the wind's howl competed with his own, freezing Percival through the layers of his sopping wet clothing, to his skin and inwards to his bones.

He stood there, far from home and all he knew, drenched and alone. The night was dark, and the narrow street upon which he found himself was sparsely-lit, much of it in shadow at best, other parts much worse than that, as though something moved in and about the dark-eyed stone facades which was more sinister, something which only came out at night.

The few figures populating this iniquitous back-alley, they smelling of cheap tobacco or cheap perfume or some ugly blend of both, negotiated their business in something akin to silence. Each knew the rules of their unspoken game, and so there was little need for speech as the players paired off, heading to places darker than the shadows, out of sight of the world.

One such figure approached Percival. "Have time for a walk, stranger? Two shillings you won't regret spending."

At that moment, a crack opened in the darkness as the moon stepped out from behind thick, black clouds. The apparition winced as though in pain at the touch of moonlight, and quickly retreated back behind the protective screen of night but, in that brief moment, Percival saw her clearly, features cast in harsh relief by the sudden, unforgiving glare.

She was a young woman, perhaps seventeen, eighteen years old, but aged beyond her years from her empty, soulless eyes to the rough, cracked landscape of her face - a face which literally bore the ragged scars of her life's experiences, with one such reaching down the length of it, from temple to chin, about a half-inch wide for much of its length. She stood before him, one thin, fine-boned hand reaching out to him, her dark eyes locked on his, confident in her skin as though she barely registered the unspeakable record of mutilation which marked her face as its domain.

She could have been pretty, Percival thought in that moment, had life and Man not abused her so. Maybe more than pretty. His eyes traversed the interrupted curve of her cheek, the graceful turn of her nose, and-

-and saw that she looked, beneath the scars and the scattered pocks, so much like his Isabelle. So much so that, but for a hundred years and the happenstance of life, the same torment of existence could have befallen she who held his heart tight within her arms. The realisation, tearing into him like the fiercest of winds, gripped his lungs tight, so that he could not breathe, not for the longest of moments, his eyes locked to hers, her gaze not leaving his, for an age, though in all good sense it could not have been more than a half-second, yet the image of her, merged with that of his love, was burned deep, deeply into the back of his eyes, remaining there even after he squeezed his lids shut over those perfidious orbs, and ran blindly into the darkness.

He ran without aim, neither knowing nor caring that he would have appeared, had any been present to witness, as though he were a madman, tearing through the night with a scream in his throat. He ran until the cobbles ran out. He ran until he could feel the sting of the spray from the furious crashing sea. He ran until he slipped, and tripped, and his forehead caught onto a rock, and the ice-cold saltwater wrapped round him tightly, and dragged him down.

And she, nameless and unknown to the world save those who walked among the same nightly shadows, and whose visage had caused such uproar on that quiet night, retreated once more away from the light, dark eyes scouting for another stranger with two shillings to spend.

**

B y the time Isabelle and the Sisters reached the bustling Black Sea port of Constanța, its muddy streets lined with the war-weary, the broken and the returning dead, they had been travelling eastwards across the continent, passing through the ever-changing landscapes of two quite disparate Empires, for almost three months. Eighty seven days, in fact, and most of them spent slogging through mud, battling the most constant rain to have been known by the natives for years, and enduring the biting chill of harsh winter nights. It had been only recently that the ice in their bones had begun to thaw, only to be replaced with a growing sense of dread as the caravan made its slow approach to the port from which they would make the final part of their journey to the Crimea, and onto the fields of battle.

Constanța, despite the faint traces of beauty which could be found in a few hidden corners among low, whitewashed homes untouched by bloody conflict and all its contagious ugliness, was a place of war. From here, supplies of munitions, food and an unending train of anxious humanity were dragged through the muddy streets to be packed aboard dark, hulking supply ships, sails cracking in the wind as though warning against the journey, to set sail across the black, Black Sea towards where Death and Chaos reigned.

It was said by those few who returned in one piece that they had initially thought Constanța to be a preview of Hell, but having made the journey to the blood-soaked battlefields and back, they saw the sprawling port, as stained with misery as it was, as a glimpse of Heaven; a blessed place, free from all of the horrors to which they had been witness.

When their caravan reached the outskirts of the port, and the cart wheels finally stopped turning, the Sisters of Barnoon Hill each said their own silent prayers into the darkness around them, soaked as it was in the din of soldiers barking orders, hawkers plying their wares and the creaks and groans of weapons and supplies being loaded aboard towering, wave-slapped ships, while the wind and the rain and the smell of fear whipped through them all.

Later, Isabelle sat with the other nurses in one of the tented canteens set up along the dockside, protected from the elements by heavy, rainsoaked canvas. They huddled closely together, partly to help keep out the cold, and partly because, now that they were surrounded by strangers rather than the familiar faces of the men who had escorted them safely across the continent for the past eighty seven days, they found themselves to be ill at ease.

In the small hours, the din eased across the port for a while, until the town itself seemed to be enjoying a moment of peace. Isabelle broke from a vertical sleep, propped up as she was by a Sister on either side. To her left, Brigitte, a full-bodied young woman from somewhere over Mevagissey way. To her right, Lily, a slight girl, barely seventeen but with a quickness of wit which belied her scant years.

Lily and Isabelle had formed a close friendship during their training, and had become quite inseparable. They had laughed together and cried together, sharing happiness and pain in equal measure. Now here, in some strange night, it half-lit by unsettling flame which created the most unnerving shadows, and with waves as black as pitch lapping at the harbour's edge, the two women were drawn closer than ever.

Isabelle leaned onto her friend's warm shoulder, closed her eyes, and returned to sleep.

For the following three weeks, Constanța was awash with bodies. The war was spreading. Catherine's army was capturing more towns to the south-west of Odesa, and her forces were massed once more at Bilhorod, laying the mighty stone fortress there to siege for the third time in ten years. Those who had fought so valiantly against the western expansion of the Russian Empire - both English and Turk - were now in retreat, or lying dead in the freezing mud.

They came in their thousands to Constanța, and to the tentative sanctuary it was able to offer. The wounded, the broken and the dead. They came from across the sea, limping in on the remnants of mighty ships, or from the north, bedraggled masses stumbling towards temporary safety on bloody, bandaged feet.

At the heart of this tortured melee, the Sisters of Barnoon Hill were the calm, gentle hands of respite; angels with cooling cloths and healing in their touch and their tone. The temporary infirmary was becoming more permanent day by day, made so by the unending nature of the flow of injured and dying men and boys. In the distance, appearing to move closer every passing day, the low rumbling of war set dread in the hearts of all.

Yet, through the fear and the suffering and the mud and the rain, Isabelle kept her spirits high, for the other Sisters if not for herself. They looked to Isabelle for strength, and she was loath to disappoint, tamping down her own fears and loneliness so as to present a visage of calm, smiling serenity to those who dearly needed it. In the back of her mind, though, she often heard the laughter of her younger sister, chiding her for being "fairy-headed still, on the inside," and it would make her smile to imagine what Mary would think of her sister should they have met there, in the blood-soaked confines of the tented infirmary at the water's edge.

One morning, the sun shone. Isabelle supposed that it had shone always, behind the clouds, hidden by the smoke from the vast encampment sprawling across and beyond the town, yet on this particular morning there was something quite wonderful about the light, as though it carried with it the promise of something beautiful to come.

Lily had been awake for some time, busying herself out in the world beyond the stained canvas walls, and had returned to the tents with fresh pails of water, to be heated for tea. Isabelle would have sworn that there was something of a skip in her friend's step, and she smiled a little, feeling that perhaps the day would be a good one, and that the new warmth in the air foretold a change of fortune for them all. Lily caught sight of her friend's smile, and passed one back in return.

"So?" Isabelle asked her friend.

"What?" asked Lily, her face a picture of faux innocence.

"You don't have to tell me, I'm sure," said Isabelle, feigning disinterest - which was enough to break Lily's composure. The younger girl rushed close to her friend, and in an excited whisper confessed "His name is Samuel. He's eighteen years old, and he's the most beautiful man I have ever set eyes on!" The pair squealed, as silently as they could, though the tent was empty save for the two of them.

"And can I assume that he has noticed you?"

Lily squealed again, barely making an audible sound but clearly conveying her excited nature. "We met at the shoreline yesterday evening, and we talked for an age! He was very much the gentleman of course, but the way he looked at me..."

At that moment, one of the other Sisters entered the tent, and the two conspirators broke rank, going about their individual tasks, each barely concealing the widest of grins.

Later, as well as jugs of tea, there were sausages for breakfast, freshly-cooked on open fires, and as the Sisters sat together, silently enjoying their unexpected breakfast treats, it struck Isabelle that the day was quiet. There were still the noises of the town, the banter of soldiers and the moans of the wounded, and still the sharp cries of hawkers and the bellowing sounds of industry, but there was something somehow lighter to the cacophony. It was, for a moment, almost a beautiful day.

But moments end, and so it was, barely an hour past breakfast, that a convoy of bodies made its slow, leaden way into the camp. Many were dead, a few close to it. Those bodies still able to walk unaided did so seemingly without sight, their gazes locked not on the road before them but on some world inside, where the guns still fired and the world shook.

**

The affair between Lily and Samuel was a beautiful thing to behold, especially amongst the horrors and devastation upon which the camp was built. Over the next few weeks, in those precious few moments between the flesh and the blood and the screaming, the couple carried out the most spectacularly obvious 'secret' romance in all of history. Somehow, they thought that their stolen glances, and the surreptitious touches their fingers made as they passed one another, were unseen by the multitudes passing through and by the infirmary. The more they tried to hide their love from view - which, perhaps, they did as a courtesy to those suffering, that it might not be seen to be distastefully flaunting their happiness - the more obvious they became. Their affair soon became common knowledge even to those patients half-dead upon their beds. One afternoon, a particularly gruff Scotsman, within kicking range of the pearly gates, summoned what strength he could, and bellowed "Just kiss her, you bloody fool!", which elicited much laughter from the audience, and flushed cheeks upon the faces of the lovebirds.

It was a fact that, rather than make others uncomfortable in their suffering, the sweet innocence of the love affair between Lily and Samuel provided a great boost for morale. To almost all those who were witness to it, such a thing - that love could blossom and be sustained in the midst of such a nightmarish hellscape - was proof of a better world to come once the war was done.

There were a few, though, who would rather sneer from the shadows than give credence to the notion that love was attainable in that place, or any place. Men so broken by the horrors they had endured that they could not conceive of a world beyond the darkness and the pain.

One in particular, a lieutenant not long returned from the battlefield, scarred and twisted in body and mind, would advance more than sneers, and in fact had for some time taken to making unwarranted advances upon Lily of a most horrible fashion, and ugly, drunken threats against her beau.

One night, in the deepest, quietest hours - during one of those times when the sins of the world were hidden by a soft blanket of darkness, and the moans of the suffering were eased, if just for a moment - Lily and Isabelle sat together around a gently-burning brazier, as the younger Sister whispered through her tears, and confided in her friend of the darkness which threatened to stain the beauty of the love between herself and Samuel.

"Poor Samuel cannot respond, though he knows the foulness of the words used by that man against me," she told Isabelle.

"Surely, there is a more superior officer to whom Samuel might speak, perhaps one to which he could plead his case, that-"

"There is no-one. The lieutenant comes from a family of some renown. He has cousins in the King's court, others in Parliament. There is not a soul here who would act against him for something so easily dismissed-"

"Dismissed?" Spat Isabelle, with barely suppressed fury. "After the foul way in which he approached you-"

"I am merely a girl, in case you had forgotten, dear Isabelle, and my Samuel is but a lowly conscript from a family of no renown whatsoever. We are, the both of us, easy prey for such as the lieutenant."

"So what will you do? You cannot live with such a burden, truthfully?" said Isabelle.

Lily leaned in closer towards Isabelle, speaking in the softest whisper. "Samuel wants us to elope. He wants us to leave here together, and to start our lives afresh somewhere without such people as the lieutenant to cause us such upset."

"Leave?" asked Isabelle, somewhat shocked at the turn of the conversation. "But, Samuel is a conscript. You may leave here of your own free will by making an offer of resignation to the Board of the infirmary, but Samuel? He will face a trial for desertion, assuming-"

"My dear Isabelle, I love you, but Samuel and I, we

deserve to be free to love, and to build a life together, do we not?"

"Of course, I-"

"Then you will keep our secret?"

Isabelle fixed her gaze to that of her close friend. "I shall take it to my grave," she said, and in the darkness of a foreign night, in the midst of a seemingly endless war, two friends embraced in a salute to love.

The following morning, Isabelle woke early from a troubled sleep, and with a leaden feeling in the pit of her stomach. A deep, anxious ball of foreboding twisted and turned inside her, but with no apparent cause. She turned to the bunk beside her, to find Lily already away, her sheets tousled and strewn across the mattress. For one brief moment, Isabelle considered that Lily had already made good on her promised elopement, but the girl would not have left her bed in such disarray, nor departed without offering a final adieu to her closest friend.

Outside, in the world beyond the canvas walls, there was a low, ominous murmuring which was growing; spreading swiftly through the air. Isabelle dressed herself quickly, apprehension turning to blind dread, and by the time she had passed beyond the canvas to the early morning air, her breathing had become horribly laboured. The murmuring flowed as a river from the infirmary down to the shoreline, and Isabelle followed it, hurrying, terrified.

A crowd was gathered at the water's edge. Isabelle pushed her way through the massed body of silent spectators until she reached its core. And there, sprawled upon the mud, lapped at by the insistent, uncaring tide, was the broken body of the young girl who right then should have been sleeping quietly in the bed next to her, as she had been on every other morning since they had settled into this ugly outpost of Hell.

Isabelle screamed - a low growl of a scream, which was ripped from the deepest part of her, and the massed body of silent spectators looked on as one young woman fell to her knees and cradled the body of another and wailed in utter devastation, while the tide jabbed at them both without ceasing.

After a long while; after the tears had stopped falling and the anguished cries had become a tortured moan, men came to take Lily away. As they did so, Isabelle spotted the lieutenant watching on, dark humour in his eyes. In the throes of an incandescent rage, Isabelle jumped up from her knees and fair flew at the man, her fingers reaching out so as to claw at his suddenly perturbed features. Men stepped in to prevent her being able to reach him, holding her back as he, smiling, turned and walked away. Though she railed at them, and loudly and openly accused the lieutenant directly of the vile slaughter of her friend, they held her fast, while their eyes betrayed their shame. As they held her still, one of the men whispered in her ear, "There's nothing to be done, miss. That is a man who will see you hang should you dare to strike at him, and there's not a soldier here not scared enough for his own life to stand against him. I'm sorry, miss."

And, just like that, Lily was gone. The following day, the lieutenant had Samuel tried, found guilty and hung for the crime of murder against the woman he loved. He went to the gallows fully protesting his innocence, and there was not one among the crowd who did not know it to be true. As the rope caught his neck, every one of them turned from the spectacle, their accusing gaze passing across the one they all knew to be guilty. They left in silence. And, just like that, Samuel was gone.

Isabelle did not watch the execution, but instead took herself away, south of the town, to a quiet, private spot along the coast, where she could be alone with her thoughts and her pain. She took along her lace bonnet, in truth the only possession she owned which had true value, or which was of any concern to her. She held it softly in her fingers as she sat watching the tide ebb and flow, eternal, uncaring, yet somehow soothing to her woes.

She had not felt quite so alone for a long time, and it cut her deeply that she could not share this with Percival. Lily's brutal, horrible death had hollowed her out, leaving her feeling numb, and empty inside, and yet, when she thought of Percival, she succumbed to a deeper level of pain, cutting into parts of her which hurt in ways she never imagined she could experience. Isabelle felt her body heave, and erupt in a most awful sobbing; an animal wailing which rang out over the silent tide, announcing to the world the pain which inhabited every part of her being.

Some time later, as the sky began to dress itself with the colours of evening, Isabelle once more ran out of tears, and she used her sleeves to wipe the traces of her outburst from her face. As she did so, a voice asked "Is there anybody there?"

Isabelle looked around her, half-expecting one or more of the Sisters to have followed her to offer comfort, or to ensure that she didn't throw her grief-stricken self into the waiting sea. But there was nobody in sight.

Once more, the voice spoke. "Excuse me, are you okay?"

Realising then in an instant where the voice was coming from, Isabelle pulled open her bonnet quickly, expecting to see the face of her beloved inside, just when she needed him so. But no. The face staring back at her was not the fair-skinned, handsome young man who had stolen her heart, but some other. An older man, pock-marked and worn by time and the sea.

For the third time, the man spoke. "I heard crying. Are you okay, miss?"

"No sir," Isabelle replied. "I'm not." And, as though it were the most natural thing in the world, as though this were just some concerned stranger who had come across a poor young woman with an aching, broken heart sobbing into the sea, Isabelle poured out her woes to the man, who sat and listened as though, for him also, this was an everyday encounter, and theirs an everyday conversation.

Isabelle told him the tale of Lily and Samuel, and of the horrific ending to their love affair. She spoke of the war, of her days at Barnoon Hill, where she first learned of the horrors of war, and made close friends she thought would last a lifetime. And she spoke of Percival, and the time at the dunes when she encountered a stranger inside a hat, and fell in love.

The man listened intently, smiling when the occasion warranted, and offering a look of quiet sympathy where appropriate. Once Isabelle had finished her tale, and her pain diminished somewhat, she asked him "And you, sir? May I ask of your story, and of how you came into possession of that most magical piece of headwear?"

The man hesitated for a moment, then admitted "This isn't my hat, miss. It belonged to a young man, I believe, who was drawn into the sea here and lost. By all accounts a pleasant young man, visiting here for a while, I'm told. Somewhat of an unhappy creature though, if the talk is to be believed."

"Oh my, that is most awful. And, if I may, where is it that are you right now? Are you in England, perchance?"

"I am indeed, miss," came the reply. "In St Ives, to be exact."

Isabelle's breath caught suddenly in her chest. She took a moment to force herself to breathe freely, and asked earnestly "Are you sure? You are in St Ives?" The man nodded in response, and Isabelle found herself overwhelmed with emotion. So many thoughts ran through her mind, too many to count, or to make sense of.

"I'm sorry, miss. Is that upsetting to you?"

"No," said Isabelle. "No, it is not upsetting, merely strange, and quite unexpected. Much more so even than speaking with another through my bonnet, if that might be believed. Please, tell me sir, what is the year on your side of this conversation?"

When the man told her the year was nineteen thirty nine, Isabelle almost screamed with delight. The man was in Percival's time! Perhaps he could help her make contact once more? She could possibly see the face of *her Percival* once more, and they would touch, and kiss, and...

"Yes, miss. That was the young man's name."

"I'm sorry?" asked Isabelle, unsure that she'd said anything to elicit a response.

"The young man, miss. You mentioned a name. Percival? That was the name of the young man who was lost at sea, miss. I only know his name because I'm a close friend of the Watts family who run the-"

"I'm sorry? What did you say?"

"Percival Ray was the name of the young man who owned this hat, is what I'm saying, miss. Though a pleasant enough fellow, he had a sense of being haunted about him, and last night there appears to have been some kind of... upset, and it seems he fell and was taken by the tide. All that remained on the shore was his hat. When I came walking along the beach this morning, I saw the thing and picked it up, and - well, there you were, miss. I'm afraid that's all I can offer on the matter."

Isabelle sat in silence for the longest time, and the man inside her hat sat with her, silent too, in respect for the young woman inside *his* hat, who seemed to be stricken with a grief of sorts, though of course he knew it would be impolite to pry-

"No."

"I'm sorry, miss?"

"No. Percival is not dead. I need you to find him for me.

I need you to place that hat in his hands, that I might see his face once more, I-" and then her words failed her, along with hope, and fresh new tears overtook her, and engulfed her.

When her tears ran dry once more, she held up the bonnet so as to ask the man for forgiveness for her outburst, but by then he was gone, and her bonnet was empty, and Isabelle was alone on a beach in a faraway land, broken, and longing only for home.

**

Everything was white. Percival tried to open his eyes, but the bright white light fought him for the longest time. When he eventually peered out at the world through the narrowest slit between his eyelids, he saw that he was in a white room, brilliantly so and filled with sunlight. His first thought was that he was in Heaven, but in the distance he could hear the sounds of sea birds, and he wasn't sure that birds went to Heaven. He allowed himself to consider the possibility that he was wrong, and that birds might have as much right as any other creature to live beyond their mortal existence. But then, what of other creatures? Did rats and cockroaches deserve to enter the afterlife? What of flies and fleas? He pondered that the number of flies which had died since time began was in all probability vastly greater than the number of human beings who had ever lived, which would mean that, should it be the case that they could enter Heaven, then the place would be thick with flies, and would be quite an unpleasant location for a person to remain indefinitely.

As his senses slowly returned, Percival became more aware of his situation. He was indeed in a white room, lying on a single bed fitted with crisp, white sheets. There were few furnishings, save for a simple white nightstand, upon which was placed a jug of clear water, and beyond that a small wooden stool, which sat beneath the open window. Beyond the window, white light had settled into cerulean blue, and within that blue a breeze, which carried to him the calls of gulls and the smell of the sea.

It was after a few moments of contemplating the fact that the sky had a particular smell that Percival noticed he was no longer alone. A young woman had entered the room, and was stood by the side of his bed. She was dressed - unsurprisingly - in white, with just a sliver of blue accenting her crisp white cap.

So. He was in a hospital. For some reason, this did not surprise Percival, though in all honesty he could not recollect why it was that he was there. He did not feel ill, nor did he notice pain from any wounds. He quietly wiggled his fingers and toes beneath the bedsheet, and convinced himself that he still retained all four limbs. The woman stood silently, watching on as Percival continued to attempt to jog his memory into doing the one job it was supposed to do, though without success.

"Good morning, Mister Ray," she said, quietly and after some moments. "I hope you're feeling well this morning?"

"I feel well indeed, thank you Nurse. So well, in fact, that I am at a loss as to why I find myself in your care."

"Hmm," said the nurse, moving towards the end of the bed, where she picked up a chart which hung from the bed frame, and began to study it. "We prefer 'S*ister*'," she said.

"Excuse me?"

"We prefer the term 'S*ister*', rather than Nurse. And this is an infirmary, not a hospital, in case you were wondering."

"How long have I been here?" Percival asked, somehow more unsure of his situation than he was before he began talking to the Sister.

"You've been in our care for about three weeks," she replied. "After you were found, you were unconscious, but otherwise in rude health, and so the doctors had you sent here for your recuperation."

"Found?"

"How much do you remember of your '*accident*', may I ask, Mister Ray?"

Her question left him both confused and concerned. "I have absolutely no recollection of any event which may have led me to be here, nor why there should have been such an emphasis placed on the word '*accident*'."

"I'm sorry," said the Sister, with apologetic sincerity. "I suppose I was merely curious as to the status of your memory and associated faculties, considering that you have been unconscious for the past three weeks or so. I meant no offence, truly. I think, in fact, that you'll find us quite a caring sisterhood here at Barnoon Hill."

As soon as he heard the words '*Barnoon Hill*', Percival's mind began to spark, as though struck by some internal lightning bolts, shocking him with pictures and emotions and realisations, though still jumbled and confused. "I know that name," he said.

"We are in St Ives," said the Sister. "You had been staying in the town for a number of weeks or so before your accident. Do you remember that?"

"I remember, I think. There was a girl..." The Sister nodded slowly, as though this made some kind of sense. "She is a colleague of yours here," Percival continued. At this, the Sister's attention was piqued.

"Really? What is her name?"

"Isabelle," replied Percival, without hesitation, "and she is the most beautiful girl in the entire world." But then, he frowned, as new images began to be imprinted on his memory. "But she isn't here now."

"Then where is she?"

"She left. For the war."

"The war?"

Percival groaned with the physical exertion of simply trying to force his memory into remembering. "Yes. She needed to go. She left with the others, and... they never came back." Suddenly, he began to remember things, things he wished he could have kept hidden from himself. Tears began to well in his eyes, and the Sister began to show signs of being concerned.

"It's okay, you don't need to remember everything at once. You should take your time. You're here to recover, and to be well."

But Percival couldn't stop the tears from coming. "They never came back," he sobbed, "not a one. The curator said so. The Sisters left for the war, and not one returned, and my Isabelle was-" and then his tears drowned out the rest of his words, and the worried young woman left the room in a hurry to seek help.

**

**

Percival slept, his dreams made of fragments of things, the understanding of which was just outside of his grasp. When he woke, he found himself on a bench, overlooking the sea. Sat next to him on the bench was one of the Sisters. Older than the one he met before, but still with the same look of genuine concern in her eyes, as though she was offering care to one of her own family. Percival thought that he remembered that he liked her, though at the same time, he couldn't quite be sure whether they had actually met.

"My name is Percival," he said, by way of introduction.

"I'm Sister Margaret, Percival. Do you not remember me?"

"I think perhaps I do, but I can't be certain."

"We've spoken many times but, because of your accident, we think perhaps your memory has suffered somewhat."

"Truly? I remember somebody telling me of an accident, though I cannot picture it. And I remember Isabelle. I think perhaps the young lady had gone to fetch her for me?"

There was a silence between them for a few moments, as

Sister Margaret composed her thoughts. All around them, the sounds of gulls and the wind and the sea.

"Percival, we have been trying to make sense of your situation for some time now, but our attempts have been thwarted by potential damage done to your memory during your accident, and a degree of resultant confusion. You've spoken to us at length of Isabelle, a young woman with whom you tell us you were involved romantically, that she was a Sister here at Barnoon Hill, and left to tend to soldiers on a battlefield, never to return. Unfortunately, though we *have* found records to support the history of such a woman, that story took place almost a hundred and fifty years ago. We think perhaps you retained elements of this story while at the old museum in town, which you had visited right before your accident."

"I think I remember these things," said Percival. And I think I remember being told of falling into the sea in some distress, and of being pulled from it by a fisherman, who no doubt saved me from a watery grave. But, for the life of me, I cannot remember what would have sent me into such a state that I would run blindly into the sea."

Percival watched a gull gliding on the air's invisible current, and thought it beautiful.

"And this is the part of our conversation where we are usually stumped. I cannot say what it was that caused you to race into the sea and put yourself in mortal danger, nor what that had to do with a story in an old newspaper from over a century ago, and you can never quite remember. We continue to be at an impasse, I'm afraid."

Percival nodded, absently. "I suppose so, Sister Margaret. I suppose so."

In the distance, the gull continued its journey to the horizon, and freedom.

**

It was a bright afternoon. Why was it that it was always so bright, he occasionally wondered - though his wondering was often short-lived, and superceded by other things which captured his attention, which could be anything from the sounds of birds to the scents caught on a playful breeze, or that time when one of the Sisters came to speak with him, and they talked for the longest while about sweet, sweet Isabelle, and Percival was sure that the lady had left to fetch her. It was bright then also, he thought.

On that particular bright afternoon though, the Sister did not arrive alone. Instead, she brought him a visitor. Percival was sat at one of the tables arranged on the balcony, overlooking the sea below.

"This is Mister Adams, Percival," said the Sister. Percival could not remember her name, but recognised her face. "He's come to visit you."

"Thank you, Sister," said Percival, and he motioned his guest to sit with him. His guest thanked him, and seated himself. The man was older than Percival, with a toughened face which suggested perhaps time spent as a fisherman, or in the navy. He was tidy, though not expensively-dressed, and he carried with him a paper bag, gripped in one hand.

They sat for a while in silence. Percival watched the gulls play in the air above the boats, while Mister Adams seemed to be trying to find a way to say something. He looked somewhat uncomfortable, almost embarrassed.

"There's no need to worry, Mister Adams," said Percival. "I may have the occasional problem remembering things, but I am quite lucid in most ways, and no danger to Man nor beast, of that I can assure you."

"Of course, of course," replied the guest.

"Do we know one another?" asked Percival.

"We do not, sir," said the other, "but I am in possession of something which belongs to you, and information which stems from that possession."

The tone in his voice caught Percival's attention. "Please, sir. Continue."

The man then set the paper bag on the table between them, and pulled from it a hat. *The* hat. Then, when he had placed that on the table also, he began to speak of how he found the abandoned Homburg on the beach after Percival's disappearance, and of how, when he'd picked it up, he'd heard sounds from within it. As Percival sat in silence, Mister Adams related the conversation which he'd had with the woman he'd met through the medium of the hat, and how she had been seeking Percival, whom Adams had thought perished in the sea.

"I heard only recently that, in fact, you had been pulled from the grave, and were in fact here, at Barnoon Hill. I came as swiftly as I could, to return this to you, and to let you know that the woman trapped within is mourning you through my error, and I can only hope that you have the wherewithal to contact her, and to let her know that you live, sir. For, it seemed to me that her love for you was a powerful thing, and if that was so, then how much more powerful her grief might be."

There was silence for a while, save for the gulls, and the whisper of the ever-present breeze. Then, after a while, Percival whispered, "You spoke with Isabelle?"

"I did, sir," said the visitor, and then he retold to Percival at length all that Isabelle had told him - of her finding her love in the most peculiar way amongst the dunes; of becoming a Sister at Barnoon Hill; of the journey to the war, and of the horrors which befell her close, cherished friend because of love. All the while, Percival listened in silence, his tear-filled eyes never straying from the hat placed on the table. That damned hat, the source of all terribleness and all wonder in his life. He remembered everything then, from that first, most beautiful kiss to the knowledge of her terrible, terrible end, and he would have sworn, had anybody asked, that he could feel his own heart break.

He cursed the hat. He cursed himself. For, were it not for his own weakness; his own over-preponderance of self-destructive emotion upon hearing of the fate of the Sisters, and of his own Isabelle in particular, he would not have been so lost as to fly into the sea, and he would not have been separated from the only means of contact with his love, and that at a time when she needed him so. He told himself that she had not deserved to have such a creature as he in her life, one so weak as to run from the darkest truth. And yet, he could not stop himself from loving her, and from craving the chance of just one more moment together with her.

At some point, Mister Adams left, but Percival barely paid him any mind. Instead, he continued to sit at the table, watching the gulls swoop and cry across the wide open sky, while cradling the stiff felt hat in his arms.

**

**

Constanța was an encampment consigned to darkness. The constant barrages from Russian cannons had reduced much of the old town to a grim mudscape, while fires - lit and kept burning for days and weeks by the enemy which almost completely surrounded them - blanketed the entire area in a thick, choking layer of smoke.

The convoys of the dead and the wounded had stopped arriving, as Catherine's troops had blocked all routes from the fields of battle to what had once been an oasis of promise. No doubt, the war was almost lost for England, but the suffering continued nonetheless. Men still screamed in pain, both of the mind and of the body, and men still caught diseases, and lost limbs, and succumbed to the ravages of unholy wounds by way of lonely deaths far from home.

Isabelle continued to tend to the needs of her charges, but with silent, stoic resignation rather than the bright eagerness for which she had been known in what seemed to be a distant past. Since the deaths of Lily and Samuel, and the learning of the passing of her most beautiful Percival, Isabelle had been drained of all but the necessary will to live and endure, that she might continue to serve her calling. But all sense of the potential for joy in life, should there ever even be an end to the hideous war, was lost to her. Every day, the guns drew closer; every day, the smoke got thicker; every day, more men died, and, through it all, Isabelle endured.

One evening, Isabelle sat by the side of a young man's bed, mopping the sweat from his broken torso with a cool, damp rag. He would die soon, she knew. She had developed a sense for such things. She could look at a man and know, almost to the hour, the time of his death. It was a skill which caused no few men to dread being consigned to the infirmary.

"The water's cool today, Mary," the young man mumbled, his mind having flown by way of fever to places and times beyond the war.

Isabelle did not care to disabuse the young soldier of his delirious notions, for at least within his fantasies he was no longer caged by a body which was soon to fail. "It is cool indeed, Harry," she said in return. "And the sun is bright."

"So bright. It reminds me of that day at the beach, when we travelled with your brothers to Brighton. Do you remember?"

"I do, my love. It was a beautiful day."

"I wish we could go there again, Mary."

"We will," promised Isabelle. "We will go there together,

just us two."

The young soldier smiled through cracked lips. "What if we were three?"

"That would be a wonderful thing, Harry."

"It would. You and me, and baby makes three, right?"

"Baby makes three, my love," whispered Isabelle.

"Mary?"

"Yes, Harry?"

"Can I tell you a secret?"

"I'm sure you can, Harry. My lips will be sealed."

"I met a man."

"Whatever do you mean?"

"I met a man. He spoke to me..." Harry trailed off.

"And, where did you meet him, Harry?" asked Isabelle.

"I met him in my hat. But you mustn't tell anybody, Mary. They'll think I'm molly-scrambled for sure."

Isabelle held her breath for a moment, so as not to betray

her shock at hearing the news that someone other than she had spoken to another person through their headwear. She looked around, and saw that the few other Sisters on duty were occupied in the same way as she, tending to their own charges, while most of the other men were sleeping. Seeing that they were not being eavesdropped upon, she leaned towards the soldier and whispered softly to him, "I'll not tell a soul, Harry. But, tell me, what kind of a man was he, that he was in your hat?"

"Ah, he was a strange fellow indeed, Mary. He spoke in such a bizarre fashion, and of the most outlandish things."

"And what was his name, dare I ask?"

"Now that you do ask, Mary, I'm not sure that I recall. It was such a brief interlude, some time ago, and if truth be told, I may have had a drink that evening, Mary. Is that a bad thing? Mary? Am I a bad person?"

"No, Harry," whispered Isabelle, "you're a wonderful man."

"Then, why did I leave you so far away, Mary? Why?"

Isabelle stroked the young soldier's face as he cried in the midst of his fevered dream, and as his breathing began to slow, she sang him a lullaby, softly, to carry him on his way. By the time she finished singing, the young man had passed, and the night was somehow colder.

Later, soldiers came to remove the body. They packed up the young man's things. As they did so, Isabelle approached one of the men - a young soldier she'd treated recently, in fact - and asked outright that she might keep hold of the soldier's hat.

"I see no reason why not, Sister," he replied, unconcerned at the unusual request. "He'll not be needing it any more now, will he?" And, with that, he and his fellow soldiers carried their comrade out of the tent, and into the smoke-filled night.

Isabelle busied herself for a while with wiping away the worst of the stains from the bed sheets, and preparing the bed for its next occupant. When that was done, she excused herself to nobody in particular, and walked out into the darkness. She held the soldier's hat close to her and, as she had recently taken to doing, carried her bonnet in a small pouch which she wore around her waist. There was a strange stirring of unbidden excitement waking and rising inside her, driving her to think thoughts she'd thought banished from her mind, while at the same time there were voices screaming in her head, and the words they were screaming, over and over in the confines of her aching skull, were "He's dead! He's dead! He's dead!"

Isabelle headed for a quiet spot out on the pocked, smoke-clouded mudscape, far enough from the infirmary to offer privacy, but not so far out as to leave her in danger from the uglier part of Man which often prowled through the darkness, looking for prey. Once she reached her spot, she stopped, and took several deep breaths. She was nervous, trembling, though she didn't know why. She had spent so long in mourning for Percival, yet here she was, acting as though there was a chance that she might meet him once again, and through another man's hat, no less. The entire notion was preposterous, and yet... And yet. There was still that growing feeling in her stomach, like the butterflies she'd felt when she and Percival first met, so long ago. Something was about to happen, she was sure of it - as sure as she knew that that poor young man was going to die.

She sat down on the mud, and withdrew her bonnet from its pouch, and held one piece of headwear in each hand. Then, not knowing what else to do, she thought of Percival. She pictured his face, his smile, the way the light shone on his skin. She clutched the hats tightly, closed her eyes, and wished...

...but nothing happened. The hats remained empty. Even after a minute. Two. For the longest time, Isabelle sat and hoped, two hats raised towards the sky, as though to invite a miracle, but the night remained as dark and cold and lonely as always.

Eventually, she lowered her tired arms, and let the hats sink down to her lap. She felt exhaustion overcome her, and she felt that, if she could just curl up in the mud, perhaps it would swallow her, and take her away from everything, and so she lay down, hats clutched to her chest, closed her eyes and waited for the mud to take her.

At some point, she must have fallen asleep. She woke to the sound of someone softly calling her name...

**

By the time he left St Ives, having boarded the coach across the country to Cambridge, Percival felt as though he had been drained of all strength, and of much hope. As if to personify his internal state, the clouds themselves turned black, and it rained heavily from Truro to clear past Oxford.

The Sisters had been hesitant to see him depart, telling him that, perhaps, his mind was still fragile enough to break once more without adequate rest and care, but he assured them that they had tended to him well enough to heal what had been broken. He considered this to be an utterly mendacious vexing of the truth, and his shame in the vexing showed, but they bade him godspeed and good health, and waved him on his way.

When he finally arrived home, dropping his travel cases onto the floor and closing the door behind him, Percival collapsed onto his bed, exhausted, as though he'd traversed the country on foot rather than endured a bone-rattling assault by stagecoach.

As he lay there, breathing loudly in the quietness of the

room, he looked around - at the walls, the few pictures adorning them, and the books and random ornaments which populated the shelves and bookcases dotted around the room - and he felt an unusual disquiet within himself, as though he were a stranger, or as if he had returned to the wrong house; the wrong life.

It was not to be unexpected, he thought to himself, the feeling of being at odds with one's life, especially following a period of tumult and turmoil such as that he had experienced the past... how long had it been? How long since that fateful Sunday, when he had encountered his destiny in the hidden heart of the Souks? Had it really been almost a full summer? The realisation scared him. To think that he had been living a life which until then had been extraordinarily ordinary, and to suddenly have found himself thrust into a bizarre, destructive, terrifying and yet at times beautiful existence would be enough to test the mental stamina of any man, but suddenly, Percival was doubtful as to whether he had passed the test. Indeed, he still cursed himself for the weakness within him which led him to self-destruction at the very moment that his love called out to him in need. Now, in his exhausted state, Percival's mind began to question itself again, flashing memories posing as dreams, and dreams posing as memories, filling the space between what had once been his life, and the new, discordant days in which he found himself.

And, with doubt burrowing deep into his fading consciousness, Percival slept.

He woke to the sound of insistent knocking at his door, and a muffled voice from beyond it, calling out his name.

He struggled to heave his exhausted body out of bed, and shuffled across to the door, calling out "Who is it?"

The reply was unexpected. "It's me. Avarice. Avarice Davies. From work. Open up will you, old friend."

Percival wrenched the door open. "Old f-? How on Earth do you consider us friends? Because of you, I-"

"I'm sorry, dear chap, I really am, but could we please do this inside? It feels rather public airing one's laundry out here."

For a brief moment, Percival seriously considered punching the wide-eyed buffoon at his door, but he quickly swallowed down his rage, and stepped aside to allow Davies to enter. All the while, his flustered mind was wondering why he refrained from hitting the fool, and at the same time was intrigued to know what had brought Avarice Davies, genial man of the people, to his home.

Maybe it was the exhaustion, maybe it was the general discombobulation he was experiencing after a summer of strangeness and infirmity, but Percival moved as though in a dream, preparing a coffee for them both, and then inviting his guest to sit with him at the table, as though these were the most natural things in the world to be doing.

After a brief moment of silence, Davies began to speak.

"I'm really sorry for the intrusion, old- Percival," he said, nervously, "but to be brutally honest, I wasn't entirely sure that I would find you... well, you know..."

"No. What?" Percival responded.

"Well, alive, of course. We, most of us, were rather of the opinion that you had.. well, that perhaps things had all become a little too much for you. And I'll admit, much of that was my fault, and I earnestly apologise, Percival. I am most deeply sorry. I was just riled so by your threat to punch me that I acted without thinking, and of course, truthfully, I know that you're not that kind of fellow, not the kind for roughness and violence, but I was put out some, and it was my foolishness and my pride which led me to report it to the Constable. I felt damnably awful about it from the start, but when things for you went from bad to worse, I must admit I have never felt such shame."

"Really?" asked Percival.

"Really. And then, when word began to spread of your..." Davies hesitated, unsure as to how to articulate his thoughts in a way which would not antagonise Percival.

"My what?" asked Percival, unnerved.

"Well, stories began to circulate, as they will in a town such as this. It seems that a number of people had spoken of seeing you, well, speaking into your hat. Full-blown conversations, as though there were a person inside it. Some assumed that these was merely drunken shenanigans, a young man playing the fool, but others considered something far more awful."

"Such as?"

"A good number of people - not myself, but a number of others - were of the opinion that what had happened to you had pushed you over the edge, that you had lost your mind and were conversing with figments of your fevered imagination."

"And you?"

"Me? I was just worried for you, old friend. I really am so sorry for the part I've played in your suffering, but I need to know that you are well, and that if you aren't, I need you to know that I will be here for you, to help you regain your sense of self, your... your sanity."

"So, you *do* think I'm mad?"

"No! Of course not. But there's no doubt that you've been through much. Word is abroad within BB's that they gave you the sack without so much as a by-your-leave, and your landlady has spoken freely to all and sundry of her decision to evict you at the end of your contract, and such things are liable to play on the mind of any man. Then, when you disappeared without a trace, and for such a while, many assumed the worst. I'm glad to see that the worst has not come to pass, but I need you to know that you are not without friends. Please, Percival, if there is anything I can do for you, you only need ask. I shall do anything of which I am capable."

Percival saw the earnestness in Davies' eyes, and realised that perhaps he had judged the fellow wrongly. There was something about his demeanour which portrayed a direct honesty, and besides, the man had nothing to gain by his unsolicited outburst. Perhaps the tribulations of the past few months were the result of a dastardly series of unfortunate events which, combined with a time-defying Homburg, had led to his current state. Perhaps Davies was not to blame.

"It's not your fault," said Percival, surprising himself. He hadn't meant to say anything, it just kind of slipped out, and then more words followed, as though through a crack in a crumbling dam, becoming an outpouring which was unstoppable.

While Avarice Davies sat nursing the luke-warm cup of coffee, his eyes widened as his host recounted a tale of a most bizarre adventure, of magical hats, furious Frenchmen and a most powerful love which endured across time itself.

"And then, when I went along to pay the man his ten

pounds, lo and behold-"

"*I* was there!"

"Indeed, and it was such an awful situation, for I could not, of course, blurt out the truth with you standing there, and I felt just so terrible lying to the poor man, but what should a fellow do?"

"I understand," said Davies, "most damnably awkward."

"And I felt so ashamed. I still do. I could see the disappointment in his eyes."

After a while, once Percival had drained himself of words, a calm, relieved silence settled within the room. The two men sat at the table, cradling cold cups as the world continued to turn beyond the window.

"Would you care for another coffee?" Percival asked.

Davies smiled. "That would be wonderful."

As Percival prepared the coffee, settling the finely ground beans on the water in the decorated Turkish *briki* before placing it over the low flame on his cooker, Davies looked around at the modest room with its sparse decoration.

"Have you lived here long?" he asked.

Percival gently stirred the warming liquid, and began to tell Davies of how he came to live in Cornbury, and to work at Battersey, Battersey & Kendrick. At first, Davies listened intently, curious to know more about this rather odd, but quite likeable chap.

But then, after a few minutes of quiet, rambling conversation, from childhood days to the time some fellow copied from Percival to cheat in the Basic Accountancy exam, Davies began to be a little distracted. He couldn't put his finger on the reason initially, but then he realised that he seemed to be hearing two conversations at once. One more muffled than the other. His eyes scoured the room, as it seemed to him that the voices he heard were coming from within the room itself. Yet, there was nobody there.

"Almost ready," said Percival, preparing the cups for pouring into.

"Damn your eyes, dæmon!" said another voice, and it was then that Davies realised that the voices he'd been hearing were coming from the somewhat dishevelled Homburg sitting on a side-table nearby.

In one furious, panic-filled moment, Percival turned back towards the table, coffee-filled cups in hand, and saw Davies staring intently at the hat. His eyes widened with the fear of some new, calamitous obscenity as Davies reached over and picked up the enchanted headpiece. As the cups slipped and fell, in seeming slow motion, thick brown liquid folding over itself in a delicate dance to the floor, Percival reached out, but in vain. Davies held the open bowl in front of him, and looked to it with terror in his eyes. Though Percival could not see the face contained within the brim, he could hear the maddened screams emanating forth. Seconds later, though it seemed so much more, as Davies stared on, petrified with shock, the hat's new tenant, affeared of the Devil's work, took to the headwear on their side of the portal with a torch, and powerful flames began to lick out to scorch the edges of the Homburg, some catching the fingers of the unfortunate fellow sat holding it.

Percival reached out quickly, grabbing the hat from Davies and rushing to the kitchen sink, where he proceeded to pour water into and around the edges of the hat. The over-zealous screaming ceased instantly, and the hat was just a hat once more, though slightly more tattered, and smelling of woodsmoke.

Satisfied that the danger had passed, Percival chuckled. "So, now you know I'm not mad, right?" he said, turning around. But Davies had already left, and Percival could hear his quickly retreating steps as he exited the building, and raced along the street.

"But, maybe that's not necessarily a good thing," he said, mostly to himself.

Later that night, Percival sat alone at his table, staring into nothing as the evening faded into night.

He was thankful that Davies had not called the Police, or worse, a Doctor. Though, in all honesty, if he had then it might have turned out the worse for Davies himself. After all, to launch a complaint against a chap for having a violent, flame-wielding zealot housed within his headwear would be enough to have the poor fellow shipped off to Bedlam before the night's end.

But, nevertheless, poor Davies had suffered something awful, and so unexpected, and yet Percival could scarce turn up at his door with a settling explanation. He had, though unintentionally, drawn that poor *bon vivant* into a world of dreadful peculiarity and frightening madness, and at the centre of this world of insanity, sat the hat. But what could be done? He could not rid himself of the offending item without losing his only possible connection to Isabelle, or to those who might pass on his declarations of love to her, and though he might face a thousand fire-bearing zealots or punch-happy Frenchmen, he knew that he would continue to suffer such for just one opportunity to see, to touch, to kiss his beloved, and to grovel at her feet for forgiveness that he had failed her in her hour of need.

And the darkness turned darker still, and the night became deep night, and still Percival sat at the table, Homburg in hand, gazing into the shadows, alone.

**

**

He woke to the smell of smoke. He jumped up, quickly scouring the shadows for a sign of flame, but there was nothing. Perhaps he had dreamt it. He sat down once again, relaxing somewhat for a moment, before realising that he could still smell smoke. Woodsmoke. It was not overpowering, but it was definitely real.

Then, his eyes made out a faint, blood-red glow in the darkness of the room. Close by. On the table.

The hat!

Percival snatched the Homburg from the table, and opened the bowl, half-expecting to see the rabid zealot reappeared, with a view to completing his labour of destruction.

And there, right in front of him, close enough to touch, was the face of his beloved Isabelle. She was sleeping, lying on muddy ground, her face stained, her clothing also, but she was as beautiful and as radiant as the first time he had laid eyes on her. The headpiece through which he was viewing her was resting on the mud, looking up at Isabelle, and in the background he could make out an encampment of sorts, barely-lit by ageing campfires, and the air all around swimming with smoke.

For a few moments, he watched her in silence, ecstatic in his soul to be there, so close, after he had thought all to be lost, including hope. Then, after a while, he whispered her name. He didn't want to scare her from her sleep, but he also didn't want this opportunity to pass them by. He whispered her name again. Her beautiful, beautiful name.

"Isabelle."

Her eyelids flickered for a moment, then opened, and without hesitation she turned and looked straight at Percival, and on seeing him she grabbed hold of the hat and pulled it close to her, and her lips were crushed against his and his against hers as though their lives depended upon it, and their worlds joined, and all that mattered was that each was there with the other, and there was no divide, just the kiss.

When finally they separated, they each spoke rapidly, one over the other, their words meshing in declarations of love, and apologies and breathless excitement.

"My darling Percival, I thought you dead," Isabelle cried, through happy tears.

"Please forgive me, my love," said Percival. "I was not there when you needed me, and I-"

"You are here now, my darling, darling man, and you are alive, and that is all that counts."

"I don't want to ever leave you again, Isabelle. If I have to fight my way through Hell itself, I will find a way for us to be together."

"There is nothing I would wish for more, my darling. Nothing. And yet, in truth, we have but this moment. The enemy draws closer here, and I fear the worst, but in the midst of all this darkness, you are here to shine a light, a most wonderful, warm and welcome light."

Isabelle reached through, and took hold of Percival's hand, and he wrapped his fingers around hers, and they each pulled the other close, through two worlds separated by the years. In each world there was a night, and a heart filled with both love and loss in equal measure.

"Speak to me, Percival," Isabelle asked. "Tell me of the life we could have had."

"Were we to have found a way past the brims of hats and caps and bonnets?"

"Yes."

"Well, I would surely have wasted no time in proposing that we be wed!"

"And I would have said yes, and delightedly so!"

"And we would be married at the church in the village where I was born, and my family would fall in love with you just as I have-"

"And we would find a way to bring my family across the country,"

"And across the years,"

"And my sister Mary would be my bridesmaid,"

"And we would move into a cottage on the outskirts of the village,"

"And would there be children?"

"There would be so many children!"

"Oh, yes, my darling," Isabelle laughed. "And we would name them alphabetically, of course."

"Of course. Alfred should be the first,"

"Or Amelia,"

"Touché. Then Blake,"

"Or Bethany,"

"Okay, yes, they shall all be girls!" Percival conceded.

"But for the one. And we shall call him Percival, after his father."

"And they will all be as beautiful as their mother,"

"And will there be chickens?" Isabelle laughed.

"As far as the eye can see! Chickens everywhere!"

And, in the darkness of two entwined nights, a pair of lovers laughed together, as though all was right with the world. They talked through every delicious moment of being together. Percival made coffee, and he passed a cup through to Isabelle, and they shared more moments drinking, and speaking of all manner of things.

At one point, Isabelle grew sombre. "May I ask you a question, my darling?"

"Of course," answered Percival.

"Does this war ever end?"

The grief which showed immediately on the face of her sweet, sweet man, how his soul seemed to crack before her eyes, told Isabelle all that she needed to know.

"I think perhaps the war will end for me, but soon, and not with victory. Am I right?"

Percival tried to speak, but he couldn't find the words, nor indeed the will, to tell Isabelle the tragic truth of her end. But, in his silence, he spoke all of that and more, and for a while the two sat, face to face, hands clenched within one another's, in loud, terrified silence.

Suddenly, the silence was shattered by a thud, and a crack, and by the earth itself being torn apart.

Isabelle turned quickly, to see her worst fears confirmed. Heralded by the violence spewed by Russian cannon, the enemy was advancing into the camp itself. Now she could hear the screams of those caught unawares by the swiftness and violence of this night-time attack. In terror, she turned to Percival.

"My love, my love, I fear I am at my end. The enemy is here, but I do not fear death if it is to be at your side, holding your hand, my sweet, beautiful man. Never let me go. Please, Percival, tell me you'll never let me go!"

And Percival could see the troops advance, with blood and menace in their eyes, and the camp was aflame, and terror and death filled the air, and Isabelle's fingers dug into his hand so deep they drew blood, but he held on tight, and told her he would never leave her, never let her go, and that she would never be alone-

and then there was a scream, and her hand was wrenched from his, and the screams and the fire and the smoke were gone, and Isabelle was gone, and Percival was once more alone, screaming his fury and pain and loss into the smoke-stained bowl of an empty, accursed hat.

**

ercival stands on the low wall surrounding the roof of the Harlequin Hotel. The birds chitter-chatter around him, unsure of this invader into their domain, but they keep their distance. The air is clear, and the blue of the sky never seems to end.

He ponders the measure of time, from one day to another; from the day he first laid hands on the hat to the day he cursed its very existence; from the day he found Isabelle in the shelter of the dunes to the night he held her hand before darkness descended, and she was taken from him.

The widow Deekes was wrong, he thinks. For all the pain he has experienced, he would gladly suffer tenfold, a hundredfold, rather than have never met Isabelle. Though the loss of her before his eyes had torn his very soul into a million broken shreds, he would not trade having known her and loved her, even though their moments together were heartbreakingly brief, for all the treasures of a lifetime. But he cannot fathom a way to continue living in a world which he did not share with her. She was the reason he existed, his only reason for being, and her name will be the last thing to pass his lips, in a whisper, as he steps off the roof...

...and in that one step, he beholds the world, stretched out before him as a tapestry beneath the bright, blue sky. And he sees each thread, wrapped around the other, never-ending, looping and crossing in infinite variety to create the most intricate patterns of life and time and being. And, in his outstretched hand, he sees the hat clearly for the first time; sees the fibres of the felt, interwoven in infinite complexity, each fibre supporting and defining the other, becoming together something vastly more than the sum of their parts...

...and the hat, in turn, sees him, and its fibres see his broken soul, and the love within it, and take pity, and suddenly the hat grows in size and wraps itself around him, until Percival is swimming within it, falling down, down into the bowl, passing easily between the boundaries of the brim, deep into the heart of the hat, where there is smoke and fire and mud, and the carnage of war - and Isabelle, his most beloved Isabelle, there amongst the carnage, fighting the darkness of unholy war as the Russian soldier beats her down.

Percival races towards her, swimming down, down deeper into the hat, closer to the battle, reaching out for Isabelle. She sees him, and screams his name, reaching out her fingers, grasping for him as he falls.

The soldier looks up, and recoils in fear, and Percival falls directly on to Isabelle, and they two together continue to fall, deeper into the hat, until there is darkness, darkness for the longest time...

...and after the darkness, the brightest light, brilliantly

white, and then the most beautiful, infinite blue, surrounding them, and the sounds of sea birds at play, and the two fall into the warm, welcoming waters of a clear, blue sea.

**

When people speak of Percival Ray, it's usually to wonder what drove him to jump from the roof of the Harlequin Hotel on that beautiful summer's day.

His subsequent disappearance is something people tend t o *not* talk about. Only a few unlucky people were witness to what happened that day, but if you were to ask them to speak honestly about what they saw, they would most probably avert their eyes, and mumble something about a man in a hat who had stepped out from a rooftop five floors above the street, and how, instead of that man's body falling to the floor, what hit the ground was a white lace bonnet, the kind that ladies used to wear a hundred years ago. But if they did say these things, they would do so begrudgingly.

They would not wish to prolong the conversation, but to hurry through it as quickly as possible, knowing that talk of such things was the stuff of foolishness, and they would in all honesty not be entirely sure within themselves of what they saw.

They would not wish to know the truth, however, for fear of being dragged into more of the same madness which had blighted their minds since that day, confusing them, and forcing them to confront the notions of their own sanity.

They would not care to know that Percival and Isabelle fell through the hat into the sea just off the coast of a small island in the summer of 1856 - the very island, in fact, where Percival's great grandfather, Elias, had been marooned for four years, before being rescued not eighteen months prior to their arrival.

They would not care to know that, after spending nine months marooned on the island, Percival and Isabelle were rescued, or that the couple, still smiling despite their endeavours, had taken passage on the boat which rescued them, had travelled with it and subsequently settled in Darwin, in the Antipodes. This, Percival suggested, would prevent them from having to explain the return of Isabelle to the world after almost sixty years without a wrinkle upon her beautiful face, and prevent also the disruption of any relationships which led to Percival having been born in the first place.

They most definitely would not want to hear of their children - Amelia, Bethany, Charlotte and Percival - or of the home they built in the country, or the many, many chickens they cared for.

They would no doubt walk away if you were to try to tell

them of all the adventures the two enjoyed together until, in the winter of 1912 - six years before Percival was born - they passed from this world to the next, within an hour of each other.

They would not hear you if you were to call after their departing ears to tell them of the headstone they shared, which read, simply :

"Percival and Isabelle Ray. A love greater than time."

**